Mystics and Medicine

Adventures in Reason

Kris Langman

Post Hoc Publishing

Chapter One

Snake Oil

SOMEBODY IN DECEPTIONVILLE was a bed-wetter. Nikki held her nose as she picked her way across the pile of wet sheets covering the stone floor. She was deep in the basement of City Hall, in the laundry room. The only light came from the embers glowing under cauldrons full of steaming water and wet sheets. A clanking sound came from somewhere in the distance, but no voices could be heard. The laundry workers had left for the day.

Nikki shivered. The room was probably hot and humid during the work day, but now that its fires were dying it was too cold for the silk tunic and jeans she had on. She still had her Westlake Debate Team T-shirt on underneath the tunic, but that was more to remind her of home than to keep her warm. She squinted into the darkness. Surely somewhere in all these piles of laundry was something she could wear. One of Fortuna's heavy velvet cloaks would be just the thing. They'd been piled in a wicker basket in the laundry cart which had carried her to City Hall. The cart had dumped its bags and baskets down a chute in the wall and she'd slid down with them. The basket containing the cloaks had rolled into a corner somewhere.

She retraced her steps back to the laundry chute and found the cloaks strewn across the stone floor. She picked one up and threw it over her shoulders. Thick swirls of embroidery covered the outside of the cloak. There were even some hard lumps which felt like jewels. It was a very flashy item of clothing. If someone saw her wearing it she might get arrested for stealing. She felt around inside the cloak and up under its hood. The inside was smooth, thick wool. She turned the cloak inside out and put it back on. The jewels dug into her shoulders, but a few scratches were better than a cell in the City Hall dungeons.

As her eyes adjusted to the darkness she noticed the faint outline of stone steps leading up out of the basement. She carefully made her way toward them, her Nikes slipping on soapy puddles and what felt like sand. She knelt down and scooped up a pinch, rolling it between her fingers. A faint ammonia smell met her nose. It wasn't sand, it was lye, an ancient form of soap made by mixing animal fat with the potassium hydroxide derived from wood ash. The laundry probably used it on the bedsheets which were heaped all over the floor. Lye was too harsh to use on things like the cloak she was wearing. And it could also burn your skin. She rinsed her fingers in the puddle at her feet and cringed as she thought of the laundry workers who had to work with the lye every day, probably without gloves. From what she'd seen of the Realm worker safety was not exactly a high priority.

She pulled the hood of the cloak over her head and slowly climbed the stone steps, listening carefully. The clanking noise was getting louder, but she still couldn't hear any voices. After two stories the stairs opened into a circular room with wooden rafters stretching high overhead. Faint rays from the setting sun came through narrow slits cut in the thick stone walls. Nikki saw at once what was causing the clanking noise: a huge hammer was crashing down onto an anvil, banging down about once per second. She glanced quickly around the room. No workers were in sight. The hammer was hard at work all on its own.

She tiptoed over to it. The hammer was pounding down onto a long strip of grayish metal draped over the anvil. The handle of the hammer was lashed to a long wooden post stretching across the room.

The other end of the post was being lifted up and down by a wooden shaft which rose up out of a dark gap in the floor. The sound of rushing water echoed from the gap. Nikki knelt down beside the gap and squinted down into the darkness. Sure enough, the waterwheel she'd been expecting to see was churning away in the depths. Deceptionville's City Hall was near the river. Part of the river must have been diverted into a channel underneath the building to power the waterwheel. The whole contraption was called a hammer mill. She'd seen a picture of one in her European history textbook back at Westlake High School. They'd been used in the Middle Ages to pound iron ore. One hammer mill could do the work of many blacksmiths. The shaft connected to the waterwheel converted the circular motion of the wheel to an up-and-down motion, just like the rotating crankshaft in a car engine moved the pistons up and down. The waterwheel could exert a lot more force than a man holding a hammer. And you didn't have to pay the waterwheel, which was good for the wheel's owner but probably put a lot of blacksmiths out of work.

The long strip of metal was also connected to the waterwheel by a system of gears. Nikki followed the snaking metal as it unrolled from a coil and scraped across the stone floor. As the strip was pulled across the anvil the hammer pounded out small disks of the gray metal. The finished disks slid off the anvil into a waiting basket. Nikki fished one out of the basket. Even in the dim light she could make out letters along its edge and a picture of something in the middle. It was obviously a coin. She was surprised to find that it bent easily. The metal was a very soft one, probably tin or lead. Strange metals to make coins out of. The only coins she'd seen so far in the Realm were gold and silver ones, but this disk couldn't possibly be made of silver. She wouldn't have been able to bend silver so easily. Silver was ranked as a 2.5 on the Mohs scale, which measured the hardness of metals. Tin and lead were only a 1.5 on the scale. Much softer than silver. And of course, less valuable. Nikki stared down at the coin in her hand. Was this just a new kind of coin, or had someone gotten the idea to make counterfeit money? A few likely counterfeiters leapt immediately to mind: Rufius, Fortuna, and Avaricious. She absent-mindedly felt the jewels sewn into the cloak she was wearing. The last time she'd seen Fortuna had been in the dungeon of the Confounded Castle in the Haunted Hills. The fortune teller had seemed desperate for money and had tried to force her to turn lead into gold. But now Fortuna was wearing cloaks decorated with jewels. She must have found a way to become rich. Counterfeiting was certainly one way to do that, as long as you weren't caught and thrown in jail.

Nikki tucked the coin into the pocket of her jeans. If she ever managed to find Fuzz and Athena again she'd show them the coin. They'd know what to do about it. But right now she had other problems. Like how to get out of City Hall without being caught by the Rounders. She looked around. Half-hidden by the waterwheel was an iron door she hadn't noticed before. It was partly ajar. She pulled the hood of her cloak farther down over her face and crept to the door, cautiously poking her head out. The door led into a long hallway decorated with tapestries and suits of armor. There was no one in sight, but she could hear voices and the clink of dishes coming from one end of the hall. Nikki took a deep breath and slid into the hallway, hugging the wall. She looked up and down. There was only one exit: toward the voices.

Sweat broke out on her forehead. She couldn't just walk into a room where it sounded like a large group of people were having dinner. Someone was sure to notice her. She was just about to slide back into the room with the hammer when she heard a man's voice coming from behind her.

"Get another basket, will ya?" said the voice. "This one's nearly full."

"Why don't we knock off for the day?" said another voice. "Me innards are so empty I could eat this here basket."

"Fortuna wants ten baskets sent to Kingston tonight and we've only got six. Yer innards'll just have to wait."

Nikki didn't wait to hear any more about the man's innards. She darted back into the hallway and headed toward the sound of clinking dishes. When she reached the end of the hall a tapestry of a deer surrounded by hunting dogs blocked the passageway. The deer had a desperate look on its face. Nikki gave it a little pat. She knew exactly how it felt. The tapestry was moving slightly, blown by air currents. Nikki knelt down and peered under its bottom edge, which was lined with tassels and dragging on the floor. She could see booted feet and the hems of ladies dresses. The feet were moving around more than she'd expected. Maybe they'd finished eating and were getting up from the table. They were conversing in loud voices. Her hopes rose. With all the movement and noise she might go unnoticed. She slowly pulled back one side of the tapestry and slid around it.

The room she found herself in was a large oak-paneled hall. It had an arched ceiling painted with fat angels lying on puffy pink clouds and grinning down at the people below. About a hundred people filled the room. Some sat at an immense oak dining table sipping wine and nibbling at cheese and grapes piled on silver platters. Others were milling around the room, chatting in small groups. There was a table loaded with dirty dishes against the wall near the tapestry door. Nikki quickly lifted the table's linen tablecloth and ducked underneath. She sat crossed-legged on the cold stone floor and peered out through a slit in the tablecloth. No one had noticed her, probably because most of them seemed extremely drunk. They were leaning on each other, sloshing the wine out of their goblets and laughing like hyenas. One lady, dressed very elegantly in a white satin gown with gold lace, spilled red wine down the front of her dress and just laughed and went on talking.

Nikki watched as waiters cleared plates and dirty wine goblets from the table and disappeared with them into a back room. At the other end of the hall was a raised platform surrounded by flags. Nikki recognized a purple flag with a golden crown in the middle. The same flag had flown on the ramparts of Castle Cogent, the residence of the King. She also recognized a forest-green flag with a circle of silver fish. She'd seen it flying on the tallest tower of the Southern Castle in Kingston. She'd also seen it on the roof of the mansion belonging to the Prince of Physics. She wondered if it was the Prince's flag or the flag of the city of Kingston. A cloaked figure stood in front of the flags. The figure's back was toward her, but it was wearing a cloak just like the one Nikki herself had on. Except the figure on the platform was wearing their cloak right-side out, with all its rich embroidery on display and its jewels glittering in the fading sunlight coming in from windows set high in the walls.

Fortuna. Nikki's eyes narrowed as she watched the fortune teller's grey-streaked hair sway across her humped back. Fortuna was talking to someone but Nikki couldn't see who it was. The person was seated and hidden from view by Fortuna's cloak. They seemed to be arguing about something. The fortune teller's arms were waving wildly in the air, her cloak flapping like the wings of a giant bird. Finally Fortuna threw up her arms in disgust and turned to face the room.

Nikki's hands clenched. Fortuna had been arguing with Rufius. He was seated in what looked like a throne. He had one leg thrown over its arm, his sandaled foot swinging lazily back and forth. His black tunic was as spotless as ever and his pale skin seemed to glow in the dim light of the hall.

Fortuna stepped to the edge of the platform and clapped her hands. The noise level lowered a bit, but it took a lot more clapping to get everyone to stop talking. Nikki grinned. Apparently the fortune teller didn't have quite as much authority as she felt she deserved.

"Quiet everyone," shouted Fortuna. "Let's settle down. I'm glad you're all enjoying the wine, which comes from my own vineyards in the Haunted Hills, but it's time to get down to business." She snapped her fingers at a waiter standing at the back of the platform. He darted behind a curtain and reappeared carrying a silver tray filled with small pots and glass bottles. Fortuna chose a midnight-blue ceramic pot from the tray and held it up.

"Lily of the Night," Fortuna announced dramatically. "The lotion in this little pot will make all blemishes vanish instantly. All age spots and wrinkles will disappear, never to be seen again. Ladies, one pot of this will make it look as if you've not yet reached your twenty-first birthday."

Several oohs and aahs sounded from the women in the room, with the woman in the wine-stained silk dress giving a loud shriek of joy, but Nikki also heard a few snorts of skepticism. One woman pointed at Fortuna's face and whispered something to her neighbor, who laughed. Nikki guessed she was pointing out that the wrinkles on Fortuna's face were so dark they looked like they'd been drawn on with charcoal. Apparently the fortune teller didn't use her own products, which made Nikki wonder exactly what was in them. She recognized the workmanship of the bottles on the tray. They'd obviously come from Avaricious's workshop. Knowing the low safety standards in his shop she had no doubt that the products Fortuna was selling contained lots of untested and probably harmful ingredients.

Fortuna ignored the skeptical snorts and put the pot back on the tray. She selected a round little bottle made of crimson glass and waved it above her head. Even the skeptic's eyes followed the little bottle as it glowed in the light of the candles which waiters were lighting in the hall.

"Panther's Pride!" proclaimed Fortuna. "Made from the thickest, richest hairs of the mighty jungle cats which roam the deepest reaches of the Southern Isles!" She uncorked the little bottle and gestured to a bald man in a purple velvet tunic who was standing in the middle of the crowd. He came forward uncertainly and twitched nervously when Fortuna poured a drop of silvery liquid onto his head. She rubbed it in vigorously. "Your head may be shiny as an egg right now, my friend, but just wait. Use this miraculous potion every day and you'll soon have the thickest head of hair imaginable. Every woman you meet will swoon at the sight of your youthful virility!"

A loud chuckle came from Rufius. Fortuna ignored him and placed the little bottle back on the tray. She dismissed the waiter and turned back to the crowd. "Friends! All of these wonderful items are now ready for sale. We are making them available to you, owners of the largest and most successful shops in Deceptionville. I guarantee that they'll generate huge profits for you. An entire room right here in City Hall is filled to the ceiling with cases of Lily of the Night, just waiting for your orders. We can ship cases anywhere in the Realm. For you, my very best of friends, I offer a discount of ten percent off the production cost. I'll actually lose money! This offer won't last long! If you'd like a chance to view our overflowing storerooms please follow me!"

Fortuna descended the steps on the side of the platform and saun-tered from the hall, her cloak swaying behind her. A few of the guests turned back to their wine goblets, but most of them followed Fortuna. Soon only the waiters, a few drunken guests, and Rufius were left. Rufius sat humming to himself, swinging his foot and smiling at some private joke.

Nikki watched him. She guessed that the carved throne he was lounging in belonged to the King of the Realm. The laundry workers whose cart she'd hitched a ride in had been talking about the King's apartments in City Hall. They'd said that Rufius was living in the apartments. It looked like Rufius was trying to take the King's place here in Deceptionville, just like he'd tried to in Kingston. In Kingston he hadn't succeeded, not yet anyway, mainly due to the power and influence of the Prince of Physics. She guessed that Rufius might have more success here in Deceptionville, which was a corrupt place and not loyal to the King, or to anyone or anything other than money.

Rufius continued to sit there, humming to himself. Nikki was beginning to wonder if he was going to stay there all night when she heard ponderous footsteps approaching. Avaricious waddled into the hall, his purple robes swishing. The fat workshop owner waved a hand lazily at Rufius, the diamond rings on his sausage-like fingers sparkling in the candlelight.

"So it went well, I take it?" said Avaricious, pouring himself a goblet of wine. "The fish took the bait?"

Rufius sniggered. "Oh yes. They swallowed the bait and most of the fishing line. These potions of Fortuna's should add a nice bit of gold to the city's treasury."

Avaricious raised an eyebrow. "To the city's treasury? So the money will go straight to road repairs, schools, and orphanages?"

"Certainly," said Rufius with a grin. "And I believe the city needs a new bridge over the river as well. We mustn't forget the bridge. Of course, you'll get your cut before the roads, bridges, and orphans."

"I'd better," said Avaricious. "And the cut had better be a big one. My workshop put many hours into making all those potions."

"Using only the finest ingredients, I'm sure," said Rufius. "Tell me, who exactly did you test these potions on? I heard a rumor that all your alchemists threatened to quit if Panther's Pride got anywhere near their scalps."

Avaricious shrugged. "Any ill effects will show up when the first customers start using the potions. We can blame any rashes, bleeding or deaths on Fortuna. She's made herself the public face of the whole scheme, after all. The public will take any complaints they have to her. And I'm sure she'll be her usual kind and compassionate self."

Rufius laughed. "Come on. We'd better go check up on her. We can't afford to have her guests wandering all over the building."

Nikki waited until she couldn't hear their footsteps anymore and then cautiously poked her head out from under the tablecloth. The waiters had all gone into the back room. She could hear them washing the dishes. She glanced warily at the few remaining guests, but they were all so drunk they were nearly unconscious. She crawled out from under the table and tiptoed to the door of the hall.

A quick peek around the door showed that she was near the main entrance to the building. A vast lobby with stone columns two-stories high echoed faintly with the sound of Fortuna's voice off in the distance. The hall was on the second floor of the lobby. No one was in sight. Nikki darted to the stone parapet surrounding the lobby and looked down. The lobby's polished marble floor glistened in the light from torches mounted on the walls. A sudden cough echoed off the marble floor and Nikki jumped, looking wildly around. There was no one on her level. She cautiously leaned farther over the parapet. It was a guard. She hadn't spotted him before because his little wooden guard hut was tucked against the wall on the ground floor, right below her.

Very slowly she untied her Nikes and took them off. She knew from a school field trip to the state capital building in Wisconsin that rubber-soled shoes squeaked on marble floors. She looked around. Three corridors branched off from the level she was on, but she didn't know which to choose. Her plan had been to get out of City Hall as quickly as possible, but she couldn't just walk out past the guard. He probably knew most of the people who worked in the building. He was sure to stop her and ask her what she was doing there. She waited, listening hopefully for sounds of snoring from below her, but no such luck. The guard seemed to be wide awake at his post. He coughed, shuffled his feet, and hummed a tune under his breath.

There was no choice. The main entrance wasn't going to work. She'd have to find another way out. She chose a corridor at random and tiptoed to it in her stocking feet, breathing a sigh of relief when she was out of sight of the lobby.

The corridor seemed to stretch for miles. She had no idea that

Deceptionville's City Hall was so enormous. She'd only had a brief glimpse of the exterior the last time she'd been in Deceptionville. She passed door after door as she went deeper into the building. Most of the rooms looked like offices, with scrolls and parchments piled on carved oak tables. There was a strong smell of candle wax, but no lights were burning in the rooms. All the workers had gone home for the day.

The cold marble floor of the corridor soon chilled her stocking feet. The room she was passing had a wooden bench just inside the door, so she ducked in and sat down to put her shoes back on. She had just finished tying her laces when a sudden movement caught her eye. She jumped up, stifling a gasp.

"It's all right, young lady. No need to be afraid. It's only me, old Geber."

Tucked away in a dark corner of the room was a very old man sitting in a chair. His long white beard reached nearly to his lap and his bald head shone in the moonlight coming in through a lead-paned window. He picked up the black cat which had been napping in his lap and place her gently on the floor. The cat hissed softly and stalked out of the room.

The old man chuckled. "Poor old Rowena. She's not getting any younger and she doesn't like having her sleep disturbed. I'm afraid you caught me having a bit of a snooze as well." He unhooked a cane dangling from the arm of the chair and slowly raised himself to his feet. "Would you like some tea, my dear?" Not waiting for an answer he hobbled over to a brick stove which had been built into the outer wall.

Nikki watched warily as he struck a piece of flint against a block of white quartz. Sparks flew into a small pile of straw nestled in a depression on the stove top. A flame soon grew and the old man added a few sticks of wood to the pile. He placed a three-legged iron trivet over the flame and put a tea kettle on top. "Hand me that pail of water, will you my dear?" he asked, pointing to a corner of the room.

Nikki glanced from the corner to the door of the room and back again. Should she run? If the old man started yelling the guard from the lobby would be up in a flash. Right now the old man was the only person who knew she was in the building. If he raised the alarm she'd have guards hunting all over the place for her. It seemed like a better idea to stay and keep him happy.

"Um, sure," she said, fetching the pail.

The old man took it from her and carefully poured water into the tea kettle. He handed the pail back. "Just put it out in the hall, please. One of the errand boys will refill it for me tomorrow morning."

Nikki took the pail out to the corridor. There was still no one in sight. She set the pail down on the floor, careful to make no noise. When she re-entered the room she saw that the old man had lit a torch on the wall. By its light she could see that the room was different from the others she'd passed. It was more laboratory than office. Glass beakers were piled on a work table and one wall held shelves stacked with glass jars full of colored powders. It reminded her of Gwen's laboratory in the basement of Muddled Manor.

"Just shut the door, will you my dear?" said the old man as he spooned tea leaves into two mugs. "Don't want that blasted Thomas up here. He's the night guard. He gets bored and likes to leave his post whenever he hears me pottering about. He drinks my tea and brags for hours about his success at dice games and his winnings at cards. Drives me mad. One of these days I swear by all the ghosts in the Haunted Hills that I'm going to poison him just so I can have some peace and quiet. And don't think that I wouldn't get away with it. Oh, I'd get away with it all right, just like that conniving young whippersnapper Rufian got away with poisoning old Mally. Not that anyone misses old Mally, of course. Likely even the King is glad he's gone. Never very popular, was old Mally."

Nikki quietly shut the heavy oak door. She doubted that the old man was dangerous. He moved so slowly, hobbling on his cane, that she was sure she could be out the door and far down the corridor before he had moved two steps. "Who's Mally?" she asked.

"The King's advisor," said the old man. "Well, he used to be the King's advisor. Dead now, as I said, and not missed. His real name was Maleficious, though I always called him Mally. We were at school together. Everyone called him Mally there. Maleficious was a ridiculous, pompous name for a little boy. And he grew up to be a ridiculous, pompous old fool."

Nikki sat down on a high wooden stool next to the workbench. "So, you think someone poisoned him, sir?"

"Call me Geber," said the old man. "Everyone does. I don't mind. I don't stand on ceremony. Sometimes they call me Mr. Geber, but *that* I do mind. Means they want something." He shuffled to the workbench, his cane hooked on his forearm, the two mugs of tea sloshing in his shaking hands.

Nikki hopped off her stool and took the mugs, setting them on the workbench.

Geber slowly lowered himself onto a stool. "Can't prove poison," he said, stirring his tea with an ink-stained quill from the workbench. "It's just my little hunch. Mally was an old man. He hadn't left Castle Cogent in years, and he died in his chambers in the castle. His death could have been due to natural causes. But I still have some old acquaintances up at the castle. People right in the inner circle of the King. They all say Mally had severe stomach cramps and vomited blood right before he died. Arsenic poisoning would be my guess. There are deposits of arsenic in caves in the Haunted Hills. People mine the deposits to use as rat poison. Pretty easy to get your hands on it. I have some of it here." He waved a hand at the shelves on the wall.

Nikki glanced uneasily at the jars on the shelves. She stared down at her mug of tea then pushed it away without taking a sip. "So, if he was poisoned, who do you think did it?" she asked.

"Rufian," said Geber, nodding his head decisively. "You mark my words, young lady. It was Rufian. Snivelling, conniving little son of a cheese-monger. He was here in D-ville when Mally died, but that doesn't mean anything. Probably bribed one of the castle servants to slip the poison into Mally's wine."

"Do you mean Rufius?" asked Nikki.

"Of course," said Geber. "Rufius the Rufian. I just call him Rufian for short. Call him that to his face, I do. He hates it. Makes him turn purple, which is highly amusing, let me tell you."

"That seems like dangerous thing to do," said Nikki. "Making Rufius mad, I mean. He's become quite powerful as far as I can tell. And he's got powerful friends, like Avaricious and the Knights of the Iron Fist."

Geber shrugged and took a swig of tea. "When you're as old as I am you don't care as much about making enemies. I suppose Rufian could have me poisoned, same as he did Mally, but so what? I'm only good for another year or two at the most anyway. Little Rufian. Oh, I have his number. He wants power. And money, but mostly power. I've met his kind before. He likes to give orders, likes to be important, likes people bowing down to him. He used to bring cheese from his parent's shop in Popularnum up to the kitchens at Castle Cogent. But he didn't confine himself to the kitchens. Oh no, not he. He chatted up every courtier in the place and took to flattering old Mally. Soon as you can blink he was Mally's apprentice. Wormed his way into the King's good graces as well. And now little Rufian has set himself up in the King's apartments here in City Hall."

"Did you know that Fortuna the Fortunate is also here?" said Nikki. "She's selling creams and potions to shopkeepers from all over the Realm. They just had a big meeting downstairs. She's showing them her storerooms full of potions right now."

Geber didn't answer. Instead he creakily raised himself from his stool and tottered over to a shelf on the wall. He picked up a little clay pot and carried it back to the workbench. "Lily of the Night," he said.

Nikki stared at it. "Where did you get it? Did you make it?"

"Of course not," said Geber indignantly. "Those two-bit hacks over at Avaricious's workshop made it. I had one of my errand boys steal me a sample so I could have a look at it. Find out what's in it."

"And did you find out?"

Geber nodded. "Oh yes. It wasn't hard. I took a bit out of this pot and heated it over an open flame. It was animal fat, mostly. Pig fat, probably from the pig farms near Kingston. To mask the smell they added bits of lavender. No need of tests for that, you can smell it with your own nose. After I melted off the fat there was a small amount of grayish powder left. I had my suspicions about that, so I mixed the powder with some vinegar."

"You were testing for lead," said Nikki. She had done something similar in her high school chemistry class, mixing a small piece of lead with vinegar and hydrogen peroxide to produce a white powder called lead acetate. Of course, in her chemistry class they'd worn gloves, aprons and safety goggles, and used lots of ventilation. And they'd disposed of the lead acetate in a hazardous waste container. She very much doubted that Avaricious's workshop was so cautious when they created Lily of the Night.

Geber raised his bushy white eyebrows. "That's right, young lady. How did you know that?"

"It was just a guess," said Nikki. "Lead used to be used in face powder. It turns the skin white. Some ladies like that, but it's very dangerous. Lead is poisonous." She poked at the gunk in the little pot with a piece of quill. "Is there enough lead in one pot of Lily of the Night to be dangerous?"

Geber stroked his long white beard. "No, not in one pot. But if a lady used say, a pot a week, well then problems would definitely arise.

She could look forward to baldness, muscle spasms, mental problems, and even death."

Nikki stared down at the little pot. "We have to tell people."

Geber harrumphed. "Do our civic duty, you mean? Save the citizens of the Realm from themselves? Not an easy task, young lady. Don't really see how we can spread the word. And even if we could, many ladies of the Realm would ignore our warnings and keep slapping on Lily of the Night. Vanity is a powerful opponent."

"It's not just the ladies who are in danger," said Nikki. "Fortuna is also selling something called Panther's Pride, which is supposed to cure baldness in men. I bet it has a few dangerous ingredients as well."

Geber shrugged. "The male of the species is just as vain as the female. I suggest you drop the matter, my dear. You won't get far trying to save people from themselves."

"Maybe not, but I think we should at least try," said Nikki. "We might be able to convince a few people that Fortuna is selling dangerous products. We could do some kind of demonstration here in Deceptionville," said Nikki. "In the main square."

Geber shook his head. "We'd be thrown in the City Hall dungeons, young lady. Before we could get one word out. I've lived in D-ville most of my life. It's always been a corrupt place, with the Rounders and the city council taking bribes right and left. But things have become much worse lately. Rufian, Avaricious, and Fortuna have been running D-ville as if it was their own private kingdom. Fat old Avaricious has always been the town's biggest crook, but after he teamed up with Rufian and Fortuna the three of them took complete control of the city council. After the mayor was found dead the council announced that all large gatherings were now illegal. No parades, no speeches, and definitely no demonstrations. And besides, your idea of a demonstration won't work. There's no way to demonstrate the dangers of lead. Not in a quick public show. Lead is a slow poison. The effects don't show up for months, even years."

"But *you* know it's dangerous," said Nikki. "I'm a little surprised by that. I didn't think anyone in the Realm knew. I met a man in Avaricious's workshop who said he'd mixed lead glazes for pottery since he was a child. He said it was harmless even though it was obvious that he had severe mental problems and the skin on both his arms was an ugly grayish-white."

Geber snorted. "I'm far from the only person in the Realm to know of lead's dangers. All of the alchemists in Avaricious's workshop know lead is poisonous. They're very careful not to handle it them-selves. They get fools like the man you met to do the dangerous work of mixing lead compounds."

"All the more reason to tell the public . . ." Nikki began.

Geber waved an impatient hand. "Sorry young lady, but I'll have nothing to do with it. A fool's errand it is. No one will listen to you and you'll just get yourself in trouble. Now, this has been a lovely chat. It's been nice to have some company other than my cat, but I think it's time for another little nap." He heaved himself off the stool and tottered back to the dark corner where he'd been dozing. Snores soon echoed around the room.

Nikki sat staring uncertainly at the little pot of Lily of the Night. As she was mulling over what to do an insistent meow came from out in the hall. She hopped off the stool and opened the room's heavy oak door. Rowena, Geber's black cat, strolled in and rubbed herself on Nikki's ankles.

Nikki scratched the cat under the chin, earning a cascade of purrs. "I have a cat, you know," she said to Rowena. "Well, she's still more of a kitten. Her name's Cation." Nikki sighed. She hoped Cation was okay. Fuzz wasn't fond of the kitten, but surely Athena or Gwen would look after her. She wondered where everyone in their little group was. Their last plan had been for Linnea to lead them by secret trails to Kingston, and then to meet up with Griff's ship. Would they stick to that plan, or would they abandon it to search for her? She wasn't sure. She knew Fuzz and Athena felt responsible for her, since they'd taken her out of her own world and brought her to the Realm of Reason. Still, very bad things were happening in the Realm right now. Rufius and the Knights of the Iron Fist were trying to seize power from the King, and imps all over the Realm were being harassed and even attacked. Fuzz and Athena might feel they couldn't put their plans on hold. After all, they had no idea where she was. It could take them weeks to find her. It might be easier for *her* to find *them*. She knew where they were heading – Kingston harbor. But the idea of trying to get from Deceptionville to Kingston all by herself was scary. Just thinking about it made her feel tired. Geber's laboratory suddenly seemed much more appealing than wandering the dark corridors of City Hall. There was a cot against one wall, covered with wool blankets. Nikki stumbled over to it, yawning. She crawled under the blankets. Rowena jumped up on the cot and curled up next to her head, purring softly. Nikki was soon fast asleep.

Chapter Two

The Wolf's Hide Tavern

"Hey! You! Wake Up. What're ya doin' in me kip?"

"Wha . . . ?" Nikki groggily poked her head out from under the woolen blanket. A boy about twelve years old was standing over her, looking distinctly annoyed. He was dressed in a rough linen shirt and pants and his bare feet were filthy. He reminded her of Curio. He had the same uncared for and un-parented look.

"Me kip," repeated the boy. "It's where I take me snoozes. You're in it." He kicked a leg of the cot for emphasis.

"Oh, sorry," said Nikki, clambering off the cot. "I didn't know."

"Don't mind him, young lady," said Geber, tottering toward them on his cane. "He's more bark than bite. And even his bark is more puppy than wolf."

The boy glared at him. "I'm plenty wolf," he said. "The blokes at the Wolf's Hide Tavern all say so. They wouldn't let me in if I weren't tough." He put his hands on his hips and puffed out his chest.

Nikki stifled the urge to laugh.

Geber waved his cane at the boy. "I've told you a hundred times, my boy. Stay away from that blasted place. Lurker hangout. That's what it is. You'll get yourself into more trouble than you can handle. Now go fetch some water for our morning tea."

The boy made a rude hand gesture and stalked out of the room.

Geber sighed. "He's not a bad boy, really. Just rough around the edges. No manners, because he had no parents to teach him any. His name is Sander. He was a pedestal baby. And like most of them he's unschooled and ill-mannered. Not their fault, of course."

"No, of course not," said Nikki, suddenly feeling less annoyed with the boy's rudeness. Curio had also been a pedestal baby. His mother had abandoned him on a stone pedestal which was somewhere in Deceptionville. She didn't know exactly where. Apparently this pedestal was used as a drop-off spot for orphans and unwanted children. Kind of like the way people would sometimes leave unwanted children at the hospital or the fire station back in her hometown in Wisconsin.

She felt a sudden longing to see her own mother. She'd been in the Realm of Reason for nearly two months now. It was very interesting and she'd made many new friends, but the flashes of homesickness were difficult to fight off sometimes. In the back of her mind lurked the horrifying thought that maybe the portal back to her own world was closed now. Maybe she was trapped here in the Realm forever. Sweat broke out on her forehead and she missed what Geber was saying to her.

"Pardon?" asked Nikki.

"I asked, young lady, whether you are staying for breakfast?" said Geber as he tottered over to the brick stove. "Our repasts aren't fancy, but we have plenty to share."

"Um, sure. Thank you very much," said Nikki, yawning and squinting at the sunlight streaming in from the window slits in the room's outer wall. She hadn't expected to sleep all night and she felt a bit disoriented. And she was still uncertain what to do about Fortuna and her dangerous, lead-laced potions.

"Just fetch a loaf of rye down if will be so kind," said Geber, waving his cane at a cupboard nailed to the wall above Nikki's head. "We keep the bread up there so the rats don't get at it, but I find it difficult to reach that high nowadays."

"Sure," said Nikki. She stretched on her tiptoes and was just able to reach the cupboard. She grabbed a fragrant loaf of dark rye bread and handed it to Geber, trying hard not to think about the rats that might have been scampering around her cot while she slept.

Geber sawed the loaf into thick slices and toasted them over an open flame on top of the brick stove. He handed a slice to Nikki. "There's butter in that little red pot on my workbench," he said. "No, wait. That's a salve I mixed for one of the blacksmiths in the market. He gets the most awful skin rashes." He peered nearsightedly around the room. "Now where did I put the butter?"

"It's over on da windowsill," said Sander, returning with a pail full of water. "I put it there meself so you wouldn't use it in one of yer potions." He poured water from his pail into an iron tea kettle on the stove and then fetched the butter, plunking it down on the workbench in front of Nikki. "She's not gonna eat all our bread, is she?" he asked, hungrily eyeing the toast Nikki was nibbling on.

"There's plenty to go around," said Geber, handing the boy a piece of toast. "You'll have to excuse Sander, young lady. He doesn't like sharing his food. Not that you can really blame him. Before I made him my assistant he was roaming the streets of D-ville scrounging for scraps in the garbage heaps."

Sander gobbled down his toast, scattering crumbs everywhere. Rowena slinked up to him and wound herself around his legs, mewling for handouts. Sander gave her a rough nudge with his foot.

"Now, now," said Geber. "No need for that, my boy. Rowena's just hungry, same as you." He offered a small piece of toast to the cat and she disappeared with it under the cot Nikki had slept on. "So, young lady," said Geber, "What are you up to today? Sander and myself will be down in the basement most of the day, making paper. You are most welcome to stay here, if you wish."

Nikki quickly swallowed the last bite of her toast. "Paper?" she asked in surprise. "I thought everyone here wrote on parchment."

Geber nodded. "Yes, parchment is the usual choice. It's durable and holds ink well. But it's expensive and only available after a cow or sheep has been killed. And the tanning process is lengthy, not to mention smelly and unpleasant. Because of its cost parchment is only available to the rich. Consequently they are the only ones who can read and write. The farmers, field hands, dairy maids, tavern keepers, fishermen and other laborers are mainly illiterate and uneducated. It makes them easy marks for greedy and power-hungry people such as Fortuna and Rufian." He paused to pour boiling water from the whistling tea kettle into three cups. He handed one to Nikki and joined her at the workbench. "Where was I? Oh yes. Paper. You see, one day last spring I happened to be browsing in the shop belonging to Avaricious. An over-priced establishment, but it carries things which can't be found anywhere else in D-ville. A large party of traders from the Southern Isles had just come into town and Avaricious was buying up all their wares. Among their spices and silks they had something I'd heard of but never seen with my own eyes. Paper they called it. Little squares of very light material. Useful for writing upon. The traders refused to reveal the secret of how it was made, but I could tell simply by its feel and smell that it was made at least partly from wood."

"Spruce and pine," muttered Sander, slathering butter on another piece of toast.

Geber chuckled. "Yes, Sander is now very familiar with papermaking, aren't you, my boy?"

"Familiar with the rough parts," grumbled Sander.

Geber clapped him on the back with an age-spotted hand. "Well, that's why you are in my employ, young sir. Because of your strong young back." He turned back to Nikki. "We have a machine down in the basement. One of my own design, I humbly admit. It is connected to a waterwheel and it does the most difficult work, that of sawing the pine boards into small pieces. Of course, the boards must be loaded onto the machine in the first place, and I'm afraid that kind of heavy work is too much for me. Sander loads the boards onto the sawing platform. After sawing another attachment pounds the small pieces of wood into pulp. Alas, my contraptions can't do everything. Not yet anyway. There are still many steps which must be done by hand."

Nikki took a sip of tea and wondered about the waterwheel contraption she'd seen down by the laundry room. She was tempted to ask Geber if he'd designed it, but decided that might not be a good idea. If it was banging out counterfeit coins then Geber might be part of the scheme. He seemed like a nice old man, but she didn't know anything about him other than that he was an alchemist. An official one, apparently, since his laboratory was right inside of City Hall. But, a nice person or not, Geber might be useful. His papermaking had given her an idea.

"Do you think I could watch you make paper?" Nikki asked.

"Of course, my dear," said Geber. "It's quite an interesting process. And if we ask him nicely Sander may even show you how we make ink. I used to buy ink from Avaricious, but his prices are ridiculous. I finally managed to figure out his formula and now I make my own. Good thing too, as the demand for paper and ink has gone sky high. It's all the proclamations, you see. There have been changes lately here at City Hall. Our mayor was recently found dead in the river and Rufian and Fortuna have taken control of his office and of the city council. They've started releasing new proclamations nearly every day. Quite full of hot air, those two are. They like to have every word of theirs written down and distributed all over town. They love to see their proclamations nailed to every door, tree, and fence post. But that got to be expensive, using stacks of parchment every day. So they came to me and I was able to provide a much cheaper solution using my new papermaking process."

"But you don't like Rufius," said Nikki. "Last night you even implied that he murdered Maleficious. Why would you want to help him?"

"Help him?" said Geber, looking baffled. "I'm not helping little Rufian. I'm just fulfilling my duties as Chief Alchemist. Sixty years I've been at my post. I've seen dozens of mayors and city council members come and go. My allegiance isn't to them, but to my post and to the city of Deceptionville."

Nikki looked at him warily. It troubled her that Geber didn't care who was in charge in his city. He might complain about Rufius in private, but it seemed that the old alchemist wasn't going to take a stand against either Rufius or Fortuna. She stuffed down her misgivings and slapped on a fake smile. "Can we go down to the basement right now? Papermaking sounds so interesting."

PAPERMAKING WAS *NOT* interesting, thought Nikki as she watched drops of sweat fall from her forehead into the vat she was stirring. Not interesting in the slightest. What it was was hard work. Her arms were aching. She rested her wooden paddle against the side of the vat and scooped up a handful of slurry. It looked like wet oatmeal. Surely it must be ready by now. She felt like she'd been stirring for hours.

"Not even close," said Sander, leaning over the vat. "Them pieces of wood needs to be much smaller, else da paper falls apart after it dries." He handed Nikki's paddle back to her. "Keep stirring," he said with a nasty grin.

Geber tottered up to the vat, one arm holding strips of cloth. "My dear, help me tear these up into small pieces. As small as you can make them. I buy these on the cheap from the weavers in town. They're leftover scraps of cotton cloth. When added to the slurry they make paper stronger than wood alone."

Nikki took the scraps and gratefully slid down onto the cool stones of the basement floor, sitting with her back against the vat.

Geber slowly lowered himself onto a little bench nearby and began tearing the scraps into narrow ribbons. Nikki copied him.

"Ow's this?" asked Sander, shoving a wooden bowl full of black liquid under Geber's nose.

Geber pushed the bowl away. "I'm not blind, boy. No need to dunk my face in it." He stirred the black liquid with a piece of broken quill. "A bit too thin, I think. Add a few more egg whites."

Sander slunk away, muttering.

"Ink," said Geber to Nikki. "My own recipe, though I admit I did have Sander hang around Avaricious's workshop while they were making their version. He heard enough to get me started before they chased him out. It's a good thing he did, as there is an unusual ingredient which I never would have thought to use. Oak galls."

"What are those?" asked Nikki.

"They are round little balls. They grow on oak trees when a wasp lays its eggs on the oak leaves. We dry them, crush them and soak them in vinegar overnight. There is some ingredient in them, some kind of acid I think, which makes ink a rich, dark black. We also soak bits of scrap iron in the gall water. Iron helps the ink last longer and keeps it from fading. Then we stir in egg whites which binds the mixture together"

The acid in the oak galls was probably tannic acid, thought Nikki. It produced the dark color when tea leaves were boiled, and it was common in the roots and leaves of some types of trees.

"Here, my dear," said Geber, handing Nikki a pair of heavy scissors. "I think we've got enough strips of cloth. Now you need to cut the strips into tiny pieces. I'd help you, but I'm afraid my days of working with scissors are over." He held out a shaking hand. The joints of his fingers were swollen with arthritis.

Nikki took the oddly-shaped scissors. Instead of the fulcrum being in the center of the two blades, as in modern scissors, these had a large ring at one end. They reminded her a bit of barbeque tongs. Instead of putting your thumb and one finger between two rings you had to squeeze with your whole hand. It was awkward, but after a few tries she got the hang of it. At the end of twenty minutes she had a good-sized pile of cotton fluff.

"That should do, my dear," said Geber. "Sandor, be a good lad and stir these into the slurry."

Sandor slouched over, grumbling. "Ain't it time for me break yet? Me bread and cheese is gettin' all dry and spoiled."

"Not quite yet, my boy," said Geber. "Just stir those in while I show our guest the rest of the process." He picked up a wooden frame which was leaning against the vat of slurry. The frame was about a foot square and covered in wire mesh. Geber dipped the frame into the slurry and shook off the excess water. What remained on the wire mesh looked like a patch of thick wet oatmeal. It reminded Nikki of the papier-mache projects she'd done in grade school.

"Follow me," said Geber. He carried the wire frame over to a trestle-table set up in one corner of the basement. "We turn it over, like so," he said, tipping the frame upside down and whacking it loudly against the table. A squishy, plopping noise came from under the frame. When Geber lifted the frame a fat square of wet mush was left on the table. Geber picked up a piece of heavy fabric and covered the mush with it. "And for now the water extraction," he said. "If you would be so kind, my dear, as to retrieve that rolling pin." He pointed under the table.

Nikki dragged it out, grunting with the effort. It was made of marble and was twice the size of a normal rolling pin.

"Now, nice even strokes, my dear," said Geber. "Up and down, then from side to side. Ten times each."

Nikki gave him a dirty look, which the old alchemist didn't notice. With great difficulty she heaved the rolling pin onto the table and began pushing it across the mush. Her shoulders strained from the effort, but she could see that the roller was working very well. Water gushed out of the mush and the small square rapidly grew much thinner and wider.

"Wonderful, my dear," said Geber. "You've made your first piece of paper. It is lacking the cotton pieces, so it will not be of high quality, still it's a good first effort. I sell the lower-quality pieces to the local schools for children to scribble on. Now, if you'll just take it into the drying room and hang it on a rack." He pointed to a small door at the far end of the basement.

The drying room was reached by a narrow stone staircase which wound around and around in a spiral. Nikki was panting by the time she got to the top. The room was many stories above the basement level of the building and had a lovely breeze blowing in from large open windows. Nikki hung her wet piece of paper on one of the clotheslines stretched across the room and stopped to catch her breath. Paper in various stages of drying hung on the lines like huge butterflies, but what caught her eye were the stacks of finished paper piled in a corner. Someone, probably Sander, had already cut the pieces into nice convenient sizes. Just right for a proclamation from City Hall. Or a carefully worded warning of the dangers of lead poisoning. It was a shame, thought Nikki, that she had such lousy handwriting. And having to write with a goose quill wasn't going to improve it. But she would just have to do her best. Now all she needed was some ink.

NIKKI SWORE AS a big blob of ink dribbled onto the paper, wiping out the word "danger" and turning the words "don't touch" into "ouch". She crumpled up the sheet and grabbed another, squinting up at the moon which was shining into the drying room from an open window. Good thing the moon was full. She had enough light to see by, just barely. From the position of the moon she guessed that it was after midnight. She'd made forty posters already. Another ten ought to do it.

She glanced guiltily at the stack of papers she'd used. It was for a good cause, but she doubted that Geber would see it that way. His handmade paper might be cheaper than parchment, but making it took a lot of time and hard work. Geber wasn't going to be happy that she'd "borrowed" fifty sheets of it. She dipped her quill in a pot of ink and carefully lettered another poster. She had two versions, one for men and one for women. The one for men said "Panther's Pride Will Make Your Hair Fall Out!" The one for women said "Lily of the Night Will Make Your Face Scabby and Red!" Neither one was very catchy, but it was the best she could do on short notice. Her first thought had been to warn of the dangers of lead, but then she realized that most people in the Realm didn't even know what lead was. Trying to explain about its chemical properties on a poster just wasn't going to work. Her best option was to make people scared to use Fortuna's potions, even if they didn't know why the potions were harmful.

When all fifty were done and their ink dry she stacked them, rolled them up, and stuffed them into a leather tube she'd found among the alchemy supplies in Geber's workshop. It looked like an old quiver for arrows. Geber hadn't noticed her take it because he'd fallen asleep in his usual chair after dinner. A long day of ordering her and Sander to keep stirring the slurry had tuckered him out, Nikki thought grumpily. The thought of Sander caused her to look nervously over her shoulder. He'd disappeared after dinner, but he'd given her a deeply suspicious look before leaving. Almost as if he knew she was up to something. She wished she knew where he was. The thought of him prowling the dark basements and corridors of City Hall searching for her made her extremely jumpy.

She pulled the strap of the quiver over her head, hid the ink pot in a corner, and fluffed up the remaining stacks of paper to hide the fact that a lot of pieces were missing. She dragged a spool of clothesline over to one of the open windows and peered over the window ledge. Far below she could hear water rushing over a waterwheel and see moonlight glinting off Deceptionville's river. The river wound around the foundations of City Hall, forming a natural moat. Directly under the window was a wooden pier jutting out into the water. A small barge and several rowboats were tied to it. Nikki guessed that supplies were brought into the City Hall basements that way.

She unwound the clothesline from its spool, measuring it with her arm, which she estimated was about twelve inches from knuckles to elbow. After unwinding the entire spool she had roughly one hundred feet of line. It would be enough she told herself firmly, trying not to think about what would happen if it was too short. The clothesline was thick and sturdy. She was pretty sure it would hold her. She tied one end to an iron hook near the window using a double bowline knot she'd learned in her sailing classes. It was a very reliable knot, unlikely to come undone as long as you tied it correctly.

She yanked on the line to make sure it was secure then threw the loose coils over the window ledge. The sight of the line flapping around in the breeze was unnerving, but she knew that would stop once her weight was on it. She took a deep breath and climbed onto the ledge, her legs swinging in the air, her hands tightly gripping the rope. She closed her eyes and eased her butt off the ledge, cringing as the iron hook creaked and groaned. She hung in the air, awkwardly twisting in the wind. Rappelling down a rope wasn't nearly as easy as it looked in the movies.

She twisted around until she got her feet planted on the stone wall, then slowly let go with one hand and grabbed the rope six inches lower. The strain on her arms was shocking. She hung on the line, arms trembling. There was no way she could manage a hundred feet of that. Use your legs you idiot, she thought. She slid her feet off the wall and wrapped them around the clothesline. She gave a sigh of relief. Much better. Her legs held up most of her weight and she found she could inch down the rope without too much strain on her arms.

She landed on the pier with three feet of line to spare and glanced up at the clothesline dangling from the drying room window. She had left an obvious trail behind her, but there wasn't anything she could do about it. She was planning on getting the heck out of Deceptionville anyway. Right after she put up her posters. They were going to make Fortuna furious, and Rufius wouldn't be happy about them either. They'd probably order a citywide search for whoever had created them. She planned on being on the road to Kingston long before the search started.

Untying the nearest rowboat she jumped aboard and tucked the oars into the oarlocks. The oars creaked as she took her first stroke but the noise from a nearby waterwheel masked the sound. She didn't have to pull hard on the oars. As soon as the little boat left the pier the current of the river grabbed it and dragged it rapidly downstream.

Nikki fought to keep the boat close to the riverbank. She didn't want to go far. The best place to put up her posters was Deceptionville's main square, which was right in front of City Hall. Looking over her shoulder she spotted a grassy bank sticking out into the river. She pulled hard toward it and soon felt the crunch of gravel under the boat. She hopped out into water up to her knees, cringing as the cold water soaked her Nikes and her jeans. Just to her left she spotted a mass of lilac bushes growing out over the water, their lovely scent drifting toward her on the cold night air. She gave the rowboat a shove and it glided along the bank until it disappeared into the depths of the bushes.

At the top of the riverbank a gravel path led away into darkness. Nikki walked on the grass beside the path to avoid the crunch of gravel and peered into the moonlit shadows. Carefully trimmed rosebushes and boxwood hedges bordered the path. The smell of gardenias tickled her nose. Ahead of her a white marble fountain shaped like a leaping dolphin spouted jets of water into the air. She was either in a park or some rich person's garden. She squinted, looking around for an exit. She couldn't afford to waste time admiring the city's roses. To her right she could just make out the towers of City Hall jutting into the sky above the trees. They were surprisingly far away. The current of the river had carried her farther than she'd thought. She headed in the direction of the towers and soon came to a high stone wall running beside the gravel path. Nikki followed the wall until it ended in an iron gate. The gate was locked, but one of its bars was bent as if an angry horse had kicked it. With a bit of twisting Nikki managed to squeeze between the bars.

She found herself on a street with dirty cobblestones and half-timbered buildings. A cat yowled suddenly and Nikki jumped. When her heart started beating again she glanced upward, trying to spot the City Hall towers. It was no use, the buildings were blocking her view. She hurried along and at the end of the street suddenly found herself out in the open. She'd come to a square with an oak tree in the middle. She shrank back into the shadow of the nearest building and peered around. Childrens toys were scattered under the oak tree. A rocking horse, wooden hoops, a few small lumps that might be dolls. A sign hanging from the building she was pressed against creaked in the cold night air. She peered up at it. Its letters were just barely visible in the moonlight: Miss Holdham's School for Elegant Young Ladies. A school was just the place for a poster, she thought, reaching behind her back and pulling the roll of papers out of their quiver. She pulled off the top paper and tucked the others back in. The school had a massive front door secured with an iron bar. Nikki tucked one of her Lily of the Night posters under the iron bar, spearing the top of the paper on a splinter sticking out. Most of the text was visible. She could only hope that someone would read it instead of just throwing it away.

She crossed the square in what she hoped was the direction of City Hall, keeping an eye out for another good place to leave a poster.

She was just turning down a side street when she heard the crackle of paper behind her. She turned to see a shadowy figure pulling her poster off the door of the school. The figure crumpled the paper and stuffed it into a trouser pocket.

Nikki was torn between anger and fear. Half of her wanted to run across the square and punch the person, the other half wanted to run away.

Anger won. Nikki folder her arms and glared at the shadowy figure as it headed across the square toward her. It kicked the little doll-like lumps scattered under the oak tree, sending them flying.

Nikki suddenly regretted her decision to stand her ground.

When the person was ten yards away Nikki realized who it was. Sander. Geber's snarly apprentice.

Sander stomped up to her, pulled the crumpled poster out of his pocket and shook it in her face.

"Ya goin' ta get yerself killed pulling a stunt like this," he said in a hoarse whisper. "Mazing ta me hows ya managed to survive this long in the Realm. Rufian'll hang ya from the highest tower of City Hall for this and Fortuna'll throw stones at yer corpse."

Sander grabbed her roughly by the arm and dragged her down a side street. Nikki twisted and kicked but Sander just ignored her efforts. "Stop yer fussing," he said. "We gots ta get under cover."

Sander pulled her toward a half-timbered building that had seen better days. The wooden beams holding up its rotting entrance were leaning like drunken sailors, and the smell of spoiled beer wafted from it in a choking cloud. The head of a wolf was painted above the door, blood dripping from its jaws. Nikki tried to dig her heels into the slippery cobblestones, but Sander just lifted her up and pushed the door of the tavern open with his shoulder.

"We're closed," said a voice. "You just missed last call. Get out."

"It's just me, Tinker," said Sander, letting go of Nikki and pulling the door shut. He bolted the door and threw an iron bar across it for good measure.

"Blast it Sander," said the voice. "I told you not to show your face in here again. Every time you show up trouble follows like a dirty smell."

A light suddenly blossomed in the dark room. The person belonging to the voice had lit a candle. He set it on the scarred wooden bar which ran the length of the room. Behind the bar glass bottles full of spirits glittered in the candle light. A copper footrest ran along the bottom of the bar, muddy with the footprints of the tavern's customers. Stacks of wooden ale mugs were piled high on the copper countertop that the barman was standing behind.

All Nikki could see of him was a bald head. He was barely tall enough to see over the bar. When he came out from behind it and walked over to them Nikki wondered if he had some imp blood in him. She was only fourteen and not particularly tall for her age, yet the barman barely came up to her shoulder. She started to relax a bit . . . until she spotted the knife hanging from his belt. It glittered in the candle light, a foot long and sharpened to a fine point. Nikki took a step back, putting Sander between herself and the knife.

"Who's this?" snapped the barman. "She looks familiar."

Sander pointed to the wall behind the bar.

Nikki squinted at the crude drawing he was pointing at. It was the face of a girl with long dark hair and a sharp chin kind of like her own. She gasped. It was her wanted poster.

The barman grunted. "So, what's the plan? You gonna turn her in for the reward?"

Nikki felt her blood turn to ice. She watched Sander as he dragged a foot back and forth across the dirty wooden floor.

Sander frowned, muttered something under his breath, stared up at the ceiling and then back down at the floor. "Thought about it," he finally said. "Temptin', it is. Reward's up to thirty gold coins. Never had even one gold coin in me life."

"So, what's the problem?" asked Tinker. "I'll fetch the Rounders. They'll tuck her up nice and cosy in the City Hall dungeons and we can collect the reward. We'll go sixty-forty. Sixty for you since you found her."

Sander didn't answer. Instead he dug Nikki's crumpled poster out of his pocket and handed it to Tinker. "She left this on Miss Holdham's front door. What's it say?"

Tinker uncrumpled the ball of paper and took it over to the candle. "Lily of the Night Will Make Your Face Scabby and Red." He gave Nikki a curious look. "That's what it says. What it means I don't have a clue. What's Lily of the Night?"

"A face cream, that's what it is," said Sander. "Avaricious's workshop made it for Miss High and Mighty herself. Miss Fortuna the Filthy."

"A face cream?" said Tinker. "Why would Fortuna want a face cream that's gonna turn her face scabby and red? It already is."

"She don't want it fer herself," said Sander. "She's got whole cases of it. She's gonna sell it in town, and all over da Realm."

Tinker frowned down at the poster, then walked over and thrust it in Nikki's face. "What is the meaning of this, girl? You working for a competitor? Got your own face cream, and you're trying to scare people away from Fortuna's?"

Nikki swatted the paper out of her face. "Yes, I'm trying to scare people away from Lily of the Night. But not because I have a competing face cream. I'm trying to stop them from buying it. It contains lead."

"Contains what?" asked Tinker.

"Lead," said Sander.

Nikki looked at him in surprise for a second, but then remembered that he was Geber's apprentice. He was obnoxious and illiterate, but he must have learned quite a lot about chemicals and compounds while working in Geber's laboratory.

"What the deuce is lead?" asked Tinker.

"It's this stuff they mixed into da face cream," said Sander. "Turns da skin white. Lots of ladies like that."

Tinker shrugged. "So? Why should we care if a bunch of upper class nitwits want to run around looking like ghosts?"

"Harmful, it is," said Sander. "Knew a guy who used to work in Avaricious's shop, stirring da pottery glazes. Them glazes had heaps of lead in 'em. Da skin on his arms turned white, which he din't mind. But then he started gettin' sores and scabs. The stuff took whole chunks outta his arms. He quit da shop before it could turn him looney. That's what he said happens to the old timers. Ya keep on stirring lead, and pretty soon ya'll start ta go soft in the head. Start forgettin' yer own name. Wander around laughin' at nothin'.'"

Nikki nodded, thinking of the disturbed man in Avaricious's workshop, though Sander's description didn't sound exactly right for lead poisoning. Lead could definitely cause a drop in IQ in children, but the laughing at nothing part sounded like something else. Maybe just alcoholism. Or maybe there were other poisons in the pottery glazes. Mercury and arsenic could cause mental issues. She sighed. One poison at a time.

"And it's not just rich ladies who'll be harmed," said Nikki. "Sure, they'll be the ones to buy Lily of the Night. I'm certain Fortuna will make the price so high only the rich can afford it. But rich people have maids and servants. I'm sure the maids try all the perfumes and potions and creams when their mistress is away. I've tried all the stuff on my Mom's dressing table. It's just too tempting to resist."

Tinker stared at her for a long minute. "My daughter is a chamber maid at Muddled Manor. She tends to the Duchess, Lady Ursula."

Nikki stayed quiet. She could see the struggle on the barman's face. On the one hand was a large reward in gold. On the other hand was his daughter's injured face and even eventual insanity.

"Right," Tinker said finally. "Here's what we're gonna do. I'm guessing you got more of those posters in your quiver, girl. Me and Sander, we're gonna nail 'em to the front door of every mansion in D-Ville. *That'll* stir up a hornet's nest. People'll be talking about this Lily of the Night stuff from one end of the city to the other. And whatever D-ville does the rest of the Realm does. If the snooty twits here decide the potion is dangerous then no one in the whole Realm will touch the stuff."

Sander stared at him in surprise.

Tinker shrugged. "What's thirty gold coins to me? The old Wolf's Hide does a booming business. I just raised the price of my ale and the customers still keep coming. My coffers are full." He snapped his fingers. "Hand over that quiver, girl."

Nikki was as surprised as Sander, but she pulled the strap of the quiver over her head and handed it to Tinker.

"Right," said Tinker. "No time like the present. I'll take half of these and Sander'll take the other half. If we hurry we can finish by sunrise."

"What abouts her?" asked Sander. "We can't let 'er go wanderin' about da city. If da Rounders catch her she'll get us all in a pile of trouble."

"I'll take her off your hands."

They whirled around. A man in a long black cloak was leaning against the bar. A hood shaded his face, but the candlelight showed a pale unshaven chin and a deep scar cutting across his mouth.

Nikki recognized the scar. It was the same Lurker who'd nearly caught her in Linnea's small village outside of Kingston.

"Blast it, Tinker," said Sander. "Don't ya ever lock yer back door?"

"Sure," said Tinker. "I lock it every night after last call. Don't do no good, though. These types can open any lock."

The scarred mouth grinned under its hood. "Yes, we can little man. We can do many things. Such as have this tavern closed down and its owner run out of D-ville."

Tinker's hand went to his knife. "Just try it Lurker. I opened the Wolf's Hide when you were just an ugly, squalling infant. No worthless piece of trash like you is driving me out of my own place of business."

The Lurker shrugged. "Fine," he said. "I won't drive you out of business. I'll just drive this into your spleen." In a movement too fast to be seen he reached under his cloak and drew out a sword.

"Whoa there," said Sander, stepping forward and holding up both hands. "No needs for that. We'll hand her over, won't we Tinker? Let's us calm ourselves down and haves us a smoke and talk it over. I gots some Southern Isle tobacco here, real good stuff." He pulled a small leather bag out of his trouser pocket and undid the string holding it closed. "Wanna sniff? I knows some gents like ta sniff it 'stead of smokin' it. Good either way."

The Lurker waved a dismissive hand at him, but Sander shook brownish powder out into his palm and held it up in front of the Lurker's face.

"Get that away . . ." was all the Lurker managed to say.

Sander blew hard on the powder in his hand, spraying it all over the Lurker's face. The Lurker collapsed on the floor in a fit of coughing and heaving.

Tinker was already running for the back door, the quiver full of posters under his arm. Sander and Nikki dashed after him. They flew through the open back door of the tavern and rushed down creaky wooden steps into a dark alley.

"What was that stuff?" gasped Tinker. "Never seen a man collapse like that just from a bit of tobacco."

"Dried pepper powder," said Sander. "Super hot. Makes yer eyes and yer lungs burn. Now follow me. Know a good place ta hide."

Nikki quickly lost track of where she was as she raced after Sander through the alleys of Deceptionville. Sander finally slowed to a walk when they reached the docks on the river.

Nikki and Tinker collapsed onto a wooden crate that reeked of fish.

Tinker was the first to catch his breath. "We can't just hide out on the docks, you wooden-headed numbskull. They'll search this area for sure."

Ignoring him, Sander put his fingers to his mouth and blew what sounded like a bird call. After a few seconds an answering call came from down the river.

"This way," said Sander.

He led them past heaps of crates and barrels piled on the docks, ready to be loaded onto river-going barges. The night air was cold and foggy, the shapes of the boats difficult to make out now that the moon had set.

"Here it is," said Sander. "On board, quick."

They followed him across a tilting board barely a foot wide which led from the dock to a barge. The barge decks were filled with bleating sheep. Sander shoved roughly on the sheep to make a path through to the wheelhouse. They climbed narrow wooden stairs up to a small cabin which overlooked the deck of the barge.

"So, what's this about?" asked a man sitting on a stool next to the wheel of the barge. His white beard seemed to glow in the darkness. "Want something, I'll bet. Money most likely. That's the only time you ever show your ugly mug down here on the docks."

"Aah, don't be like that, Willy," said Sander. "We just needs a little ride, is all. Just a day's ride down to da next village. You can let us off there and that's the end of it."

Willy snorted. He got down off the stool with great difficulty, his joints cracking. He shuffled up to Tinker and peered at him. "Well, here's a surprise. The barman from the Wolf's Hide. Never seen you down on the docks before."

Tinker shrugged. "Fancied a cruise down the river at night. Very romantic it's supposed to be."

Willy chuckled. "Romantic, eh? And who's this? Your new girlfriend? Little young for you, ain't she?" He leaned in toward Nikki.

Nikki jumped back in alarm. "Of course not! He's kidding. We just need a ride down the river. We need to get out of Deceptionville."

"Out of D-ville, hmm?" said Willy. "Fugitives are you? Who you running from? More to the point, how much is a ride worth to you?"

"Ah, come on Willy," said Sander. "Don't be gouging us. Just one day's ride. That's all we want. We'll help clean da decks. Bet yer crew ain't too eager to clean up sheep poop. C'mon, do me a favor. One pedestal to another."

Willy snorted. "One pedestal to another. You bring up that blasted pedestal every time I see you. It's wearing thin."

Sander just stared at him silently.

"All right, all right," Willy finally said. "One day's ride down to the next stop. That's Newton on the Water. Dull little town. Don't know why anyone'd want to go there. But what you do there is your business. Don't want to know about it. Seems like you've got yourself in a mess, and the less I know about it the better. Go down below decks until we leave port."

"Thanks Willy," said Sander. "I'll bring ya some of that salve what Geber makes next time I'm down on da docks. That stuff what helps yer achy joints."

"The Pedestal Club sure comes in handy sometimes," said Tinker as they climbed down the stairs into the hold. "Must be nice to belong to such an exclusive club. All the best people in D-ville belong."

Sander ignored him and stretched out on one of the sleeping bunks attached to the wall of the barge.

"What's the Pedestal Club?" asked Nikki.

"Tinker just means all us pedestal babies," said Sander, crossing his arms on his stomach and closing his eyes. "All us what was left on the pedestal in D-ville when we was born. Willy was left there too. Course, that was like a hundred years ago. Willy's da oldest old-timer there is. But all us pedestal babies get ta know each other, no matter how old they is. Word gets around about us. People like ta gossip, and your Ma leaving you on da pedestal cause she didn't want ya is juicy gossip."

"Oh," said Nikki, falling silent. There didn't seem to be anything to say. She thought about little Curio, who was also a pedestal baby, and tears filled her eyes. She supposed the D-ville pedestal was better than nothing. Surely some of the babies got adopted. But remembering the bits Curio had told her about his childhood, it seemed more like he was dragged into slavery than adopted. His master had beaten him and worked him very hard. Something similar had happened to Sander, though at least Geber didn't beat him, and the work in Geber's laboratory didn't seem that brutal. Nikki sighed and curled up on one of the bunks. She fell asleep dreaming about her mother making her an Angel Food cake for her tenth birthday.

Chapter Three

━━●●◆●◆

Down the River

T HE SUN WAS streaming in through a porthole when Nikki woke. She sat up and peered through the thick glass. The view was fuzzy, but she could tell they'd left Deceptionville behind. Across the river was a pretty countryside of fields and small patches of forest. Cows grazed in the fields and ducks swam in the reeds lining the riverbank. Nikki was a bit surprised she hadn't woken up from the engine noise when they'd left the dock, but then she remembered that the Realm had no engines. The boats were powered by sails, or like this barge they just floated down the river with the current. She wondered how they got the barge back up the river to Deceptionville.

She hopped off the bunk and climbed the stairs to the deck. At the top of the stairs she came face to face with a sheep. It had wandered away from the others and was staring down the stairs into the hold. Nikki cautiously gave it a shove, but it didn't budge.

"You got to push a lot harder than that, Miss," said a member of the crew who was passing by the door to the hold. "These lunkheads don't take a hint." He bent down and gave the sheep a powerful shove with his shoulder. The sheep bleated in a complaining sort of way and ambled slowly off to join the others.

Nikki made her way through the maze of sheep to the bow of the boat, where Sander and Tinker were sitting with their feet dangling

41

over the water.

"Morning," said Tinker. "Have some breakfast." He tore a hunk off a loaf of bread and handed it to her.

"Thanks," said Nikki, sitting down on a rolled up fishing net. "How long will it take to get to the next stop?"

"Couple of hours. Newton on the Water's not far from D-ville. It'd be even quicker if we didn't have to go through the locks."

"The locks?" asked Nikki.

Tinker nodded. "The Sea Canal locks. Barge traffic don't follow the river after D-ville. The river bends and heads to the Haunted Hills and gets so shallow and rocky that boats can't get through. You probably ain't heard of the Sea Canal, being a foreigner."

Nikki tensed, staring at Tinker warily.

Tinker waved a dismissive hand at her. "Don't worry, I'm not gonna turn you in to the Rounders. Know you're a foreigner cause of your accent. Also cause I've had your wanted poster up on the wall of my tavern for a month now. As I was saying, they built the Sea Canal in the time of the King's grandfather. Quite a feat of building, it was. They had better builders and thinkers back then, so they say. The King's grandfather was keen on book learning and opened hundreds of schools all over the Realm. Trained thousands of builders, drafts-men, and stonecutters. They used to call us the Realm of Reason. Even the poor could read back then. We've gone backwards since those times. Now only the children of the rich go to school. A real shame it is. Anyway, the Sea Canal branches off this river right before Newton on the Water. The canal runs all the way to Kingston."

All the way to Kingston, thought Nikki. That would solve her problem of how to meet back up with Fuzz and Athena. Floating down the canal seemed much easier than trying to find her way over land. "Do you think the captain of this barge would let me stay onboard all the way to Kingston?" she asked.

Tinker peered at her. "Maybe. If you clean the decks to earn your passage. Willy says these sheep are going to the market in Kingston. There'll be a load of sheep dung to shovel."

"I can do that," said Nikki.

Tinker shrugged. "All right, I'll ask him. But you'll be on your own. Me and Sander are getting off at Newton on the Water. We're headed back to D-ville. We'll lay low for a while and keep out of sight of the Rounders, but it's our home so we're going back. We should be all right. Both of us have a bit of power in our corner. Geber's got a lot of pull in D-ville on account of being the official city alchemist. He'll look after Sander. And I have my pet Lurkers. The old Wolf's Hide is a Lurker hangout. They've been coming there since my grandfather owned the place. I bribe a few of them with gold from time to time and they mostly leave me alone. I'll have to watch out for that one who waved a sword at us, but if I throw a bit more money around I think I can keep him under control. Besides, we have to go back. We still have to nail these to every mansion in D-ville." He shook the quiver strapped to his back.

"You're still going to do that?" asked Nikki.

"Of course," said Tinker. "I'm just a tavern keeper and Sander's just an apprentice, but we aren't gonna stand by and let people get poisoned by the likes of Fortuna and Rufius. And speaking of poison, this lead stuff, is there any cure? I've seen others like the one Sander mentioned. The one who worked in Avaricious's workshop stirring the pottery glazes and who went looney. You see them around D-ville, laughing in a strange way and talking to themselves. Most of them have burned-looking skin on their arms. My guess is most are glaze makers."

"I don't think there's any cure," said Nikki. "I'm sorry."

Tinker's shoulders drooped and he turned away, staring into the water.

Nikki chewed on her piece of bread and wracked her brain, trying to dredge up anything she could remember about lead poisoning.

Everything she knew about it was from a documentary she'd seen on TV. The lead got into bone marrow somehow. The two elements, lead and calcium, were chemically similar, and the body mistook lead for calcium and used it to build bones. Lead also got into the brain. In her world the standard way to check for lead poisoning was to do a blood test, but that kind of medical test was way more sophisticated than anything available in the Realm. Once lead affected the brain there was nothing which could be done, but the documentary had mentioned something called chelation therapy, which could pull lead from the bones into the bloodstream. Then the kidneys filtered the lead from the blood and when the patient urinated the lead left their body. Chelation therapy wasn't really a cure. It couldn't fix brain damage. All it could do was prevent further damage. The therapy consisted of a drug called EDTA injected into the bloodstream.

Nikki sighed. It was so frustrating having knowledge from a world more advanced than the Realm. Especially when it came to knowledge of medical cures which could relieve suffering. She wished she could help, but concocting EDTA was impossible. She didn't even know what EDTA stood for, and even if she knew she'd need modern laboratory equipment to make it. This wasn't like the painkilling drug she'd made from coca leaves back in Linnea's cottage. That had been a simple distillation. No, there was nothing she could do about a cure, but she could still help get the word out about the dangers of lead poisoning. Once she got back to Kingston she'd talk to the Prince of Physics about it.

"Make ready!" one of the crew suddenly shouted.

Nikki looked up. The crew was bustling about, herding sheep into the middle of the deck and unwinding thick ropes.

"Locks ahead," said Tinker, pointing.

Nikki stood up and held onto the railing. Ahead of them a sharp point of land jutted out into the river. On one side the river rushed around the point and headed towards a line of dark hills far off in the distance. On the other side was the lock, a long stone-lined rectangle with gates at both ends. As they floated nearer Nikki could see that they were miter gates. The same kind of canal gates invented by Leonardo da Vinci back in 1497. The two gates came together at a forty-five degree angle, and the edge where they joined pointed upstream so that the force of the water helped push them tightly closed.

As the barge approached two lock keepers on each bank pushed on heavy beams attached to the top of the gates. The gates swung slowly apart and the river water rushed in, pulling the barge into the lock. Once they were completely inside the barge crew threw ropes up to the lock keeper on the starboard side. He tied the barge tightly to his side of the lock to stabilize it as water continued to flow in, raising the barge until it was level with the top of the lock. Once the lock was full the lock keepers closed the gates the barge had entered by and walked to the other end of the lock to open the forward pair of gates. The barge slowly sank again as water rushed out. The lock keepers untied the barge and it floated through the forward gates and into a long earthen-banked canal which stretched as far as the eye could see.

They floated down the narrow canal which was barely wide enough for two barges to pass. They met several barges coming toward them and Nikki finally learned how they got the boats back to Deceptionville. By mule power. Teams of mules and oxen were hitched to the upstream barges with ropes as thick as her arms. The animals walked patiently along the towpath at the top of the earthen bank, doggedly pulling their heavy loads. The upstream barges reeked of fish, and Nikki could see piles of cod, halibut and tuna on the decks, their scales glinting in the sun. They were species which lived in the ocean. Probably caught by the ships in Kingston harbor. Maybe even by Griff's ship. That's where she'd head, if she made it to Kingston. Even if the imps weren't there Griff and Kira would help her.

"Make ready!" shouted a crew member, breaking into her

thoughts.

The crew set large wooden oars into openings on the deck then rowed backwards against the current to slow the boat down. Through a gap in the chestnut trees which bordered the canal Nikki could see the rooftops of a small village.

"Well, this is where we leave you," said Tinker. "Be careful in Kingston. I hear Rufius is in power there now."

"Lotta trouble you started," said Sander, scowling at her. "Better if ya stay outta D-ville."

They pushed their way through the sheep to the side of the barge. There was no pier or landing. The crew merely pulled in their oars and the barge slowly scraped against the side of the canal. Tinker and Sander stood on the railing and jumped across the two-foot gap to the towpath.

Nikki watched them disappear into the trees and wondered if she should talk to the captain about a ride to Kingston. The crew were busy with their duties and didn't pay any attention to her. It didn't seem like they cared whether she was on board or not. Maybe they were used to giving rides to the local villagers. She decided to just stay out of their way and not approach the captain unless she had to. She swatted a sheep which was nibbling on the hem of her tunic and took a seat on the railing, dangling her feet over the water.

They floated peacefully down the canal for several hours, passing farms, fields, patches of forest and small villages. After nearly falling asleep on her perch Nikki checked the position of the sun. It was about noon, she decided. Her stomach growled. She hadn't had anything to eat since the bread in Geber's laboratory the day before. A wonderful smell floated up the stairs from the hold. The crew were cooking lunch. Some kind of stew, Nikki thought, her mouth watering. She hopped off the rail and pushed through the sheep, hesitating at the top of the stairs. Raucous voices and loud laughter floated up with the cooking smells. The bitter smell of ale was also in the breeze.

As hungry as she was, she couldn't quite bring herself to go down into the hold. At times like these she missed Athena and Fuzz terribly. She liked the imps and thought of them as friends, but it was also very useful to have companions who knew the local customs. Especially when you were trapped in a realm far from your own world. Nikki sighed and returned to her seat in the bow.

A few hours later the first windmills began to appear. They sprouted from the fields like giant wooden flowers. The land surrounding this section of the canal was very flat and smaller canals began to branch off from the main line, each leading to a windmill. Up ahead Nikki could see a stone pier jutting out into the main canal. The oars came out again and the crew slowed the barge. When they were close to the pier they pulled in the oars and a crewman hopped out, tying the barge to the pier and laying down a small wooden ramp.

A line of crewmen came out of the hold, each carrying a large sack on his shoulders. They marched up the ramp and along the towpath, heading for a nearby windmill.

"Grain," said a voice behind Nikki.

She turned to find Willy the captain standing next to her. Her impression of him as very elderly wasn't mistaken. His long white beard reached nearly to his belt buckle and he leaned on a cane with a shaking hand. The look he gave her was neither friendly nor hostile.

"It's wheat from the lands belonging to Muddled Manor. It'll take us a while to get it all out of the hold. We take it over to that big windmill to grind it into flour. The Duchess of the Manor has mills on her own land. They could make perfectly good flour for her ladyship, but she insists on shipping it down here. Says these mills grind much finer and smoother." He snorted. "Don't know about that, but she pays well so I don't object. We'll be docked here for the rest of the day. You can go ashore if you want. Just don't stray too far. We'll be leaving at dusk. Next stop is Kingston."

"About that . . ." began Nikki.

Willy waved a wrinkled hand. "Not to worry. Tinker gave me a gold coin to pay yer passage all the way to Kingston. Just stay out of the crew's way when they're working."

Nikki nodded, relieved that she wouldn't have to find another way to get to Kingston. And even more relieved that she wouldn't have to shovel sheep poop all the way. She made her way over to the pier side of the barge, waited for a gap in the line of men trudging along with their burdens, and darted up the ramp. She wandered along the towpath for a while, passing an occasional fisherman casting his line into the canal. She didn't have any clear plans for the rest of the day other than to scavenge some food if she could find some. She wished Fuzz was with her. He'd probably convince the nearest fisherman to give him his entire catch and then cook it to boot. Unfortunately she didn't have the imp's talent for scrounging a meal. If she got desperate she could ask Willy the captain for some food. He seemed reasonable enough.

She tried to ignore her growling stomach and left the towpath to follow one of the little side canals. A line of poplar trees grew along the bank, their leaves rustling in the breeze. Tiny frogs occasionally plopped out of the canal and crossed her path before disappearing into the trees. Up ahead she could see that the canal was heading toward a windmill, its canvas sails turning slowly in the breeze.

As she approached she could hear grinding and clunking noises coming from an open door halfway up the wooden base of the windmill. Nikki climbed a narrow staircase up to the door and peeked inside. The big barn-like structure held a confusing array of wooden gears and shafts. Nikki was so absorbed in trying to figure out how the whole apparatus worked that she didn't notice the little red-headed girl until she felt a tap on her arm.

Nikki jumped backwards, nearly falling down the stairs. She grabbed the handrail just in time.

"Sorry, Miss," said the girl. "I didn't mean to startle you. Are you here to see my Pa? He's down at the grinder. The flour for the bakery's nearly ready." She pointed down to the floor of the windmill where a giant millstone was revolving around a vertical wooden shaft. Clouds of flour dust were billowing up into the air. A man covered head to toe in flour was holding a gunny sack up to a chute which spat out a stream of flour. When the sack was full the man quickly tied it off with a piece of string and grabbed an empty sack from the pile next to him. A pile of full sacks was loaded on a nearby wagon.

Nikki shook her head. "No, I was just passing by and was curious about your windmill. It looks like you're doing a really booming business."

"Oh yes, Miss," said the girl, who looked about nine or ten years old. She put her hands in the pockets of her flour-covered blue dress. "We sell more flour than any windmill in these parts. That's cause of my Pa. He's an expert builder. He built this windmill. It's the only one which can be adjusted to the wind. The other mills round here have to sit idle and can't grind flour if the wind's in the wrong direction. But our windmill can move its sails to face the wind. See up there, at the very top? That big wooden platform, shaped like a circle, with wooden gears? That's what moves the top of the windmill. It can move in any direction. The sails are connected to it by that shaft."

Nikki looked where she was pointing. A horizontal shaft nearly a foot thick pierced the roof of the windmill and connected through a series of wooden gears to the vertical shaft which turned the millstone.

"Come down and meet my Pa," said the girl. "He loves showing off his windmill." She headed down the stairs without waiting for an answer.

Nikki followed her around the side of the windmill to an opening on its ground floor big enough for the flour wagon to pass through. They perched on a couple of wooden barrels off to one side while the girl's father finished filling all his empty flour sacks. Once the last sack was full he pulled a lever above his head which disconnected the spinning millstone from the vertical shaft which powered it. Gradually the millstone came to a halt and the interior of the windmill was quiet except for the occasional creak of the sails far overhead.

The miller threw the last sack of flour onto the wagon with a grunt and turned to face them.

The girl jumped off her barrel. "Pa, this is . . . um"

"Nikki." Nikki hopped off her barrel and offered her hand to the man.

He wiped his flour-covered hand on his flour-covered shirt and shook hands. He was about to say something when he was wracked by a sudden fit of coughing. He bent over with his hands on his knees, his whole body shaking.

The little girl rushed over to him and patted him on the back. "He gets these fits sometimes. More and more often lately." She pulled a handkerchief out of the pocket of her dress and handed it to him.

The man coughed into it and Nikki was alarmed to see red spots appear on the handkerchief. "Maybe he should lie down," she said.

The man straightened up, waving an impatient hand. "I be all right, young Miss. Been coughing like this since I was your age. A common thing it is, for millers to have the cough. Nothing to worry about."

Nikki glanced from his pale face to the spots of blood on the handkerchief to the clouds of flour dust still floating in the air. There definitely *was* something to worry about, she thought. It was the lead problem all over again. People harming themselves through ignorance of health risks. Constantly breathing in the flour dust had to be causing some kind of lung disease. "Maybe you're right," she said. "Maybe there's nothing to worry about. But just in case, don't you think it would be a good idea if you and your daughter wore masks when the millstone is grinding? So you don't breathe in the flour?"

The man waved away this suggestion. "Had a miller try that years ago. He looked a right fool with that thing on his face. Got laughed out of our village. He had to move to Deceptionville and take up the blacksmith trade."

"Well, your daughter should wear one, at least," said Nikki.

"Everyone would laugh at me," said the little girl.

Nikki looked at her seriously. "It's better to be laughed at than to cough up blood the way your father does."

The miller looked down at the handkerchief in his hand and then at his daughter. "Aye," he said. "You may be right. So used to the fits, I am, that I forget I wasn't born coughing. Hard to believe the flour is harmful. Good home-grown wheat, it is. Healthy to eat."

"But not healthy to breathe," said Nikki.

"Maybe not," said the man. "But you'd have a hard time convincing the millers round here of that. They'd think it unmanly to run around wearing silly masks. And nobody wants to get laughed out of town. But the young ones are a different story. My little Mina here has been spending more time in the mill lately. Been training her how to set the sails. She's got quite a knack for knowing wind direction. Course, she can't lift the flour sacks, so she doesn't work the grinder and breathe the dust as much, still I might ask my wife to make her a mask."

"But Pa . . ." began Mina.

"No buts, Miss. Now, let's head home right quick. Time for the noonday meal. Your Ma will be in a tizzy if we're late. And you come along too, young Nikki. You look like you could use a good meal."

Nikki followed them along a path bordering a wheat field until a village appeared, its crooked half-timbered houses leaning precariously over a canal. The miller's house was perched on the edge of a small weir built across the canal. The water rushing over the weir turned a waterwheel, but instead of a smooth flow of water over the blades an odd jet of water shot out at each revolution. The wheel was also twisting back and forth on its axle, banging against the side of the canal.

"Pa, the wheel's broke again," said Mina. "Three blades are missing this time."

The miller sighed. "Every week I fix that thing, and every week it breaks. If we had a better way to water our vegetable garden I would give up on it and chop the whole thing up for firewood."

Nikki crouched on the edge of the canal and watched water pour onto the waterwheel. It was an overshot wheel, just like the one in Kingston in the gardens of the Prince of Physics. The wheel was located below the top of the weir and gravity sent the water crashing down onto the top of the wheel. As the water hit the blades the wheel revolved. This wheel was smaller than the Prince's, but as far as Nikki could tell the design was the same, except for one thing. The Prince's waterwheel had blades which were angled sharply back toward the falling water. This wheel had blades which were perpendicular to its axle, which meant that the water hit the full surface of each blade with tremendous force. Rather than powering the axle the kinetic energy of the water was being wasted. It was no wonder the blades were breaking off.

She was about to mention this to the miller, but hesitated. If he'd built the waterwheel it might hurt his pride to be told the design was flawed. She didn't want to make him angry. And she especially didn't want to make him angry before she'd gotten some food. She'd tell Mina after lunch. She stood up and followed them through a vegetable garden where they were growing cabbages and runner beans whose graceful vines wound around tall wooden stakes.

"There you are! It's about time! My biscuits are burnt to a crisp and the soup has gone cold!" A stout woman with greying red hair shook a wooden spoon at them. She was wearing a gingham dress and an apron with stains all over it.

"My fault, all my fault," said the miller, planting a kiss on the woman's cheek. "Never mind the biscuits Mary. Just slice some bread and cheese. We have a guest." He drew a reluctant Nikki forward to face the woman's waving spoon.

"A guest? A child, more like." She lowered the spoon and patted Nikki on the cheek. "Haven't seen you around here, my dear. What are you doing in our part of the Realm all alone? Well, never mind. Time for questions later. Sit yourself down at the table. Mina, get the bread and the pot of lavender honey which Mrs. Wilton just dropped off. It's in the larder."

Minutes later they were all busily munching on thick slices of homemade bread, chunks of cheese, and a gooey cherry tart topped with whipped cream. The miller's wife kept eyeing her curiously, but Nikki avoided her gaze. She tried to think of a good reason for why she was wandering around the countryside on her own. Somehow she didn't think telling the truth was a good idea. For all she knew her wanted poster was hanging up in the local tavern. She decided that a story about visiting a cousin in Deceptionville was believable. And now she was just paying a barge captain to bring her back to her family in Kingston. Fuzz and Athena were (hopefully) in Kingston, and they were the closest thing to family she had in the Realm, so she was sort of telling the truth.

The story proved to be unnecessary, however. As soon as the meal and the dishes were done Mina took Nikki by the hand and dragged her outside.

"There are chores to be done, young lady!" shouted the miller's wife. "Where are you off to?"

"I'm just gonna show Nikki my boat," yelled Mina. "Besides, I already fed the chickens."

"There are more things that need attending to than chickens!" yelled the miller's wife as Mina crawled through a loose board in the fence surrounding the vegetable garden.

Nikki followed her through the fence and along the main street of the village. She felt a little guilty. "Maybe we should go back and help your mother with the chores. It's the least I can do after she fed me lunch."

Mina just waved an impatient hand. "I'll do the chores later. I want to show you my boat. It's brand new. Pa just finished it. It's a beauty. He got the ballast just right this time. It was a bit off-center on my old boat and it made the boat heel too much in high winds. That's why it capsized and sank to the bottom of the lake. Pa says it capsized cause I was out in rough weather when I shouldn't have been, but that's just nonsense. I'm the best sailor for miles around. A bit of rough weather is nothing to me."

Nikki checked the wind a bit nervously. The branches of nearby trees swayed lightly in the breeze so she relaxed a little. She was a sailor herself, though not a very good one yet. She had only started lessons last year. Sailing in rough weather wasn't something she wanted to experience. Not again. Her sailing instructor had taken her out once in high winds and deliberately capsized the boat so that Nikki could practice righting it. Nikki had swallowed half of Lake Mendota before she got the boat upright. Ever since that day a light breeze was her idea of the best sailing weather.

The main street of the village eventually turned into a dirt path which wound through a grove of pines. Squirrels and blue jays chittered up in the branches and rabbits dashed into the undergrowth when they approached. When they arrived at the lake it was much larger than Nikki had expected. To the right it ended in a swampy area full of reeds and marsh grass and dragonflies, but to the left it stretched farther than she could see. Across the lake were hills covered in pine woods and behind the hills were tall, snow-covered mountains with rocky peaks which glowed in the sun. They were the first mountains Nikki had seen in the Realm.

"Pretty, aren't they?" said Mina when she noticed Nikki staring at them. "They're the Mystic Mountains. Round here we just call them the Mystics. Pa says they're the tallest mountains in the whole Realm.

He says he climbed them when he was a boy, but Ma says he just went over the lowest pass. You can see it, just there, between those two peaks. If you go over the pass you'll end up in the Trackless Forest, and if you find your way through that you'll end up at the sea. Pa didn't go nearly that far. He just went into the mountains on a dare and came right back the same day. But he likes to tell that story cause not many from our village have gone even that far. The Mystics don't have ghosts the way the Haunted Hills do, but they're still pretty strange. They say a group of hermits lives way up on one of the peaks. The hermits dance around bonfires and do all kinds of strange rituals. Some people in the village say they even do human sacrifices, though Pa says that's just village stories meant to scare little kids."

Mina crossed a pebbly beach on the lake shore and stepped onto a small wooden dock jutting out into the lake. A tiny sailboat, barely ten feet long, was tied to the end of the dock. The name "Mina's Newest" was painted on the stern.

"That's just Pa's little joke," said Mina, pointing to the name. "On account of this is my fourth boat."

"What happened to the others?" asked Nikki.

Mina shrugged. "Well, the last one capsized and sank, like I told you."

"And the other two?"

"They might have sunk, but that's not important. Help me get the mainsail up."

Nikki glanced at the lake, wondering just how many boats were at the bottom of it. But Mina gestured impatiently at her, so she climbed somewhat reluctantly into the tippy little boat and helped Mina raise the mainsail and secure it to the boom.

"I don't often use the jib," said Mina, handing Nikki a rolled-up canvas sail, "but since there's two of us today we might as well. It hooks onto the front halyard."

Nikki attached the jib and took her place in the bow, a jib rope in each hand. She didn't mind being relegated to crew. Working the jib sail was easier than being captain. As captain Mina had to work the tiller and the mainsheet, which was the rope which controlled the mainsail. The captain also had to keep an eye on wind direction and chart the course. All the crew had to do was to align the jib sail with the mainsail, changing its setting to port or starboard whenever the captain tacked or jibed.

Mina untied the bowline from the dock and they were off. They glided slowly at first, the breeze barely filling the sail. But as Mina headed toward the far side of the lake a strong wind suddenly rushed down from the mountains and their mainsail billowed out. Mina pulled in the mainsheet to close haul position and the tiny sailboat darted forward.

Nikki adjusted the jib to match the mainsail and took a deep breath as the cold wind blew over her. Spray from the lake dashed her face and she smiled. It was quite exhilarating rushing along the blue water, with the dark pine forests and rocky mountain peaks coming closer and closer . . . yikes! Nikki dropped the jib ropes and clutched the side of the hull. They were racing toward the shore of the lake and a big boulder was dead ahead.

"Tack!" yelled Nikki. "We're going to hit!"

Mina just laughed and kept going.

Nikki crouched and braced for impact, but at the last second Mina swerved into a tack, the boat heeling nearly vertical. They missed the boulder by inches and headed back out into the middle of the lake.

"That's just my practice boulder," said Mina, the wind whipping her long red braids. "I always see how close I can get. I'm up to twelve inches. The water's real deep there even though it's close to shore. Next time I'll see if I can make it six inches before I tack."

Nikki was too busy trying to catch her breath to answer. She gathered up the jib rope again and adjusted the sail, ducking under the boom as Mina jibed suddenly. They were going downwind now, with the wind behind them, so Mina let out the mainsail and Nikki set the jib to match. As she watched the mainsail billow out Nikki was glad there was no spinnaker on the little boat. The winds in the middle of the lake were very strong and Mina was such a little daredevil that she'd probably set the spinnaker even in a hurricane. Spinnakers were probably called something different in the Realm, but the principle would be the same as a spinnaker on a sailboat on Lake Mendota back in Wisconsin. When sailing downwind you rigged another sail to the front halyard which ballooned out and could greatly increase your speed. Spinnakers could only be used when the wind was behind you. In an upwind position, when the wind was coming at the bow of the boat, they just collapsed against the mast and made a mess unless you had an apparatus which could furl them quickly.

Even without a spinnaker they were picking up a remarkable amount of speed for such a small boat. The mainsail was getting a large amount of lift. Nikki's sailing instructor had told her that it was just like the lift achieved by the wing of an airplane. But this type of lift drove the boat forward instead of lifting it up into the air. The lift was created by unequal air pressure on either side of the sail. The sail had more air pressure on the windward side, the side the wind was pushing on. And less air pressure on the leeward side, the side away from the wind. Lift was created by pressure perpendicular to the wind direction, and the curve of the sail helped to create the perpendicular pressure.

"Who's that?" Mina shouted suddenly, breaking Nikki's train of thought.

Mina jibed, swinging the boat around so that it faced the village side of the lake. She brought the boat into irons to slow it down and pointed toward the dock they had left from. A mass of horses and riders were milling around the dock and the pebbly beach.

Hair rose on the back of Nikki's neck. The riders wore black tunics and armor which glinted in the sun. She was certain she recognized some of the riders. These were Knights of the Iron Fist. And all of them now worked for Rufius as far as she knew.

The boat was drifting slowly toward the dock.

"Quick!" shouted Nikki. "Turn around!"

"Why?" asked Mina, glancing uncertainly from Nikki to the riders. "Who are they? Do you know them?"

"Yes," said Nikki. "And they know me. Head for the opposite shore. As far from the village as possible. You can drop me off and I'll hide in the forest."

Mina gasped. "You can't go into that forest. You'll get lost in the mountains. No one ever goes there. I told you, there's nothing over on that side of the lake except a bunch of hermits way up on a mountain peak and they might not even be real."

The boat was drifting within shouting distance of the dock. A knight on a giant Palomino whose front hooves were at the very edge of the dock yelled something at her. One hand rested threateningly on his sword.

Nikki scrambled back to the stern where Mina sat and grabbed the tiller away from her. She swung the boat around and pulled in the mainsheet until the sail caught the wind.

Mina moved up to the bow, watching her warily. Finally she picked up the jib rope and adjusted the jib so that it also caught the wind. The boat picked up speed, rushing back toward Mina's practice boulder.

Nikki looked over her shoulder. Some of the riders were picking their way through the marshy end of the lake, but she could tell it was slow going. The horses were sinking into the mud. She would have a big head start once she got to shore, but she'd be on foot. She'd have to find a place to hide, because once they got past the marsh the horses would quickly catch up to her.

When they were close to Mina's boulder she dropped the mainsheet so that the sail luffed and the boat drifted into shore. When she heard the keel crunch along the bottom of the lake Nikki scrambled to the tip of the bow and jumped as far as she could, landing on the sand to keep her Nikes dry. The last thing she wanted was wet shoes while she was busy getting lost in the mountains.

"I think this is a really bad idea," Mina said from the boat. "I'm sure my Pa can talk to these riders, whoever they are. He's an important person in the village. They'll listen to him. You don't need to run away."

"Yes, I do," said Nikki. "Now, listen. Sail back to the dock, but don't land until you see your parents or some of the other villagers. Most of the riders should leave and follow me, but some might stay behind in the village. I want you to tell them that you don't know me. You just met me a few hours ago."

"I *did* just meet you a few hours ago," said Mina.

"Exactly," said Nikki. "Be sure to tell them that. And tell your parents thanks for lunch." She darted across the beach and into the pines. Once she was hidden among the trees she paused to make sure Mina had left. The little sailboat was slowly making its way back across the lake, with Mina looking back at the spot where Nikki had disappeared.

Nikki turned away from the lake and headed deeper into the forest. She groaned inwardly as she realized how steep the shoreline was. It seemed as if the foothills of the mountains rose right out of the lake. She was soon gasping for breath as she grabbed at bushes and tree roots to pull herself uphill. A tall granite outcropping jutted up in front of her like a giant rock-climbing wall and she scrambled up onto it. From its top she had a view of most of the lake. All of the riders had left the dock. There were a few stragglers on the beach and a large crowd of villagers was gathered around them. The riders were ignoring them, so it looked like neither Mina nor the villagers were in any danger.

She looked in the other direction. The lake stretched for at least a mile, but she could just make out the far end off in the hazy distance. But her hopes of walking around the lake and making her way back to the canal were dashed as she studied the shoreline. The beach was narrow and littered with dead branches, but the sandy strip was wide enough for a horse to walk along it. And it extended all the way down to the end of the lake. The riders would catch up to her in no time if she followed the shoreline. There was no choice. She had to head up into the mountains.

Chapter Four

The Mystic Mountains

NIKKI GLARED UP at a blue jay which was screeching at her from a pine branch above her head. The bird seemed to be mocking her for getting lost so quickly.

Her plan had been to follow the lake from half a mile inward from the shoreline. But the trees were thick and the ground rough with little hills and valleys which she had to go around. And each little hill was ringed with prickly holly bushes which scratched her hands and ripped her tunic. For the first hour she stopped frequently to climb a tree to check the location of the lake. But this quickly became exhausting, and fear seized her when the sound of horse's hooves and men's voices echoed across the water. They were getting closer. The louder the voices got the farther up into the mountains she climbed.

She was trying to climb a tall fir tree to check her location when it happened. Her foot slipped and she found herself crashing down through the branches, desperately grasping at anything which would stop her fall. She hit the ground with a thud, feeling the shock vibrate through her whole body. She barely had time to be grateful for the thick pile of fir needles which had cushioned her fall, when suddenly she felt herself falling again. The ground beneath the tree had given way and was collapsing underneath her. Clouds of dust clogged her throat and she gasped for air as she felt the earth rumble and slide.

She was caught in an underground avalanche of dirt and rock. It carried her deep under the earth.

The landslide seemed to last forever. When it finally slowed to a halt Nikki lay half buried in dirt as small rocks bounced around her. She lay still for a long time, afraid any movement would set the earth rumbling again. Finally she slowly wormed one arm out from under the dirt and brushed the dust out of her eyes. She had expected to see pitch blackness, but to her relief the rockslide hadn't carried her as far underground as she'd thought. The cave she'd been carried into was dimly lit by the sun shining through a crevice high above. She squinted up at it. Tree roots hung down from it like twisted chandeliers. A squirrel scampered down a long thick root, peering at her as if wondering why she was just lying there. Nikki stuck her tongue out at it.

She slowly got to her feet and spit out a mouthful of dust. Above her the sunlight streaming in was painfully comforting. She wanted badly to reach it but the opening was at least a hundred feet above her. She cautiously approached one wall of the cave and dug a small handhold into the dirt. The little hole immediately collapsed, the dirt crumbling into a tiny avalanche of dust. The sides of the cave were too unstable to climb. She'd bring the whole cave down on top of her if she tried.

Nikki sighed, sneezed out some more dust, and reluctantly turned to face the darkness behind her. As her eyes adjusted to the dim light she could see that the cave was bowl-shaped, with only one exit at the far end. It looked like a tunnel. She picked her way across the rubble on the floor of the cave, gave one last look behind her, then slowly walked into the darkness, one hand on the tunnel wall. The crumbly dirt walls of the cave soon turned into hard granite. Nikki could feel small, rectangular ridges cut into the wall. Pick-axe marks, she guessed. This wasn't a natural part of the cave. Someone had deliberately carved out a tunnel. As she went deeper in and the floor of the tunnel sloped downhill Nikki began to wonder if being caught by the riders might not be so bad after all. She could shout for help and they might hear her and throw a rope down to pull her out of the cave. But then she thought about the dungeons of Castle Cogent and the tiny cell she and Athena had shared, with its smell of sewage and its cockroaches. Nope, a dark tunnel with an unknown end was definitely better than a dungeon. She went on, wincing as the last light from the cave faded. She closed her eyes and felt her way forward. For some reason that was better than staring into the blackness. It gave her a small sense of control.

After stumbling along for what seemed like an hour but was probably only a few minutes she began to notice the rotten-egg smell of sulfur. At first she sniffed in alarm, wondering if the tunnel air was poisonous. But then she noticed that the smell was coming from a specific spot on the wall, not far from her. She backed up a few paces and felt along the rock face. Just above her head a small niche had been carved into the wall. Wooden sticks were stacked inside it. She pulled one out and sniffed at it. Yep. This was definitely the source of the smell. It was sulfur and something else vaguely familiar. Garlicky. Phosphorous, maybe. It could smell like garlic. The chemicals had been mixed together with some kind of gummy substance and painted on one end of the stick. Suddenly something from her AP chemistry class leapt to mind. On a hunch Nikki scraped the gummy end of the stick against the rock wall. Sparks shot out and the stick turned into a brightly burning torch.

The sticks were matches. Well, a rough equivalent anyway. Boyle. That's who she'd been thinking of. In the 1600's an Irish chemist named Robert Boyle had experimented with mixing sulfur and phosphorous together to produce a crude match. Boyle was regarded as one of the founders of modern chemistry and was famous for Boyle's Law, which stated that the inverse relationship between the pressure and volume of a gas was a constant.

Nikki gathered up all the sticks from the niche and tucked them under her arm. Holding her new torch aloft she proceeded with a bit more confidence. The wood of the torch felt springy, as if it had been cut recently. Whoever had made the matches had done so within the last few days. So that must mean the tunnel was used regularly. She couldn't decide if that was a good thing or a bad thing. It depended on whether the people who used the tunnel were friend or foe.

She crept quietly along, holding her torch. Her plan was to snuff it out in the dirt of the tunnel floor if she heard anyone approaching. But she met no one. She passed more niches full of sticks, but couldn't carry anymore. It didn't seem necessary anyway. The niches were built into the wall every hundreds yards or so. After she'd gone roughly a mile her torch began to sputter. The gummy substance was almost gone. Nikki dropped it in the dirt and scraped a new stick against the tunnel wall. It took her three more sticks to reach the underground river.

Nikki had heard the sound of rushing water before she reached the river. It echoed along the tunnel walls for the last hundred yards. When she reached the river she realized that the tunnel had come to an end. There was no bridge and nothing across the water from her but a blank stone wall. At first she thought she was going to have to turn back, but then she noticed a small path winding down to the river. She followed it to the water's edge and saw that someone had built a wooden platform jutting out into the dark stream. A flat-bottomed boat, more raft than rowboat, was tied to the platform. A set of oars was stowed in the boat.

She stood at the river's edge, looking up and down. Both directions led off into darkness. She dropped one of her sticks into the water and watched it zoom out of sight to her left. The current was very strong. Probably too strong for her to row against. Well, that decided it, she supposed. To the left it was. She climbed into the boat, piled her sticks in the bow, and untied the rope holding it to the platform. The current caught the little boat immediately, knocking her off balance. She fell hard onto the floor of the boat, dropping her torch into a puddle. It sputtered and went out. The boat raced along in the darkness, Nikki holding onto its sides for dear life. The little boat was tippy and she was afraid she'd fall overboard if she tried to reach her pile of sticks in the bow. She gave up on that idea and crouched down, keeping her head low so she wouldn't bump it against the tunnel ceiling.

The river rushed on for what seemed like miles. Nikki's hands grew cramped from holding on but she was too scared to move. The spray which blew into her face was icy cold. If she fell in she'd get hypothermia within minutes. She was a strong swimmer, but even the best swimmers would drown if their body temperature got too low. Her one comforting thought was that the boat had to be going somewhere. Whoever had tied the boat to the platform used this river to travel. There had to be a destination eventually. She just had to be patient.

Nikki squinted, trying to see into the darkness ahead. Was she imagining it? Was the darkness getting just a little bit lighter? She raised her head a few inches and peered past the bow.

Yes! A dim light shone in the distance. She couldn't tell what it was, but it got brighter as the boat raced toward it. When the boat was a few hundred yards away Nikki realized that she was looking at daylight. The river was coming out of its underground tunnel. She heaved a sigh of relief and relaxed her grip on the sides of the boat. She wasn't going to drown in an icy underground river after all.

The current seemed to increase as the boat approached the daylight. That was odd, Nikki thought. Surely the river would have room to expand once it exited the stone tunnel. The current should be slowing down. She barely had time to ponder this when suddenly the boat shot out of the tunnel. Nikki closed her eyes against the shock of the bright sunlight after hours spent in a dark tunnel. She heard a loud sound of rushing water and felt a heavy mist on her skin. She was just cautiously opening one eye when suddenly the boat dropped out from under her. She felt herself falling and falling as huge roaring columns of water surrounded her. The impact when she hit the pool far below was crushing. She fought against the roiling, boiling water as it tossed and turned her as if she was a sock in a washing machine. As she lost consciousness her last thought was of her mother standing at a workbench in her chemistry lab.

NIKKI RETCHED AS a stomach-full of water rushed out of her onto the dirt floor. She had no idea where she was. She was too busy vomiting up river water to notice much about her surroundings. After endless dry heaves she finally collapsed onto her back, her breathing raspy and desperate. She felt like she'd never get enough air into her lungs.

"Here, girl. Sit up. You'll breathe easier."

Nikki felt rough hands force her into a sitting position. Sitting up brought on another round of vomiting.

"That's right. Get it all out. The faster you recover the faster we can get you out of our land."

Nikki wiped her mouth and scrambled away from the speaker. The wobbly cot she'd been laying on tilted, nearly dumping her on the floor.

"Whoa, there. No need to look so alarmed. We might not want you here, but we aren't going to hurt you." A man stood in front of her with his arms crossed. He wore a grimy tunic and ragged trousers. He was middle-aged, with a weather-beaten face and a long brown beard. "So, our little welcome mat didn't agree with you, did it?" The man grinned. "You should count yourself lucky. Not many who go over the falls survive. You're only alive because our Headman ordered us to pull you out. Mostly we just wait until the body washes up on shore and then we bury what's left. But the Headman shows mercy to children. We get one every couple of years. They go exploring in the mountains, get lost in the caves and stumble into one of our tunnels. All our tunnels eventually lead to the falls. Better than a guard dog, they are."

"But don't you go over the falls too?" asked Nikki.

The man waived an impatient hand. "Of course not. We row hard to the right just before the falls and leave the river. There's a small inlet inside the tunnel where we tie up the boat. Then we go down the Long Stairs. They were carved inside the mountain ages ago. No one knows by who."

Nikki stood up shakily. She could feel spots on her back and shoulders where new bruises were sprouting. She'd probably hit a rock while being churned in the pool below the waterfall. She felt nauseous and short of breath, but the man was right. She was lucky to be alive. She looked around her. They were in a cave with wet stone walls and a strong smell of mold. Fortunately this cave wasn't deep underground. One wall of it was open to the outside. She could feel a fresh breeze and see a grove of birch trees waving in the wind.

The man beckoned to her. "Come on. The Headman asked to see you as soon as you were awake. He's the one who decides whether to let you go."

Nikki didn't like the sound of that but she realized she didn't have much choice. She followed him out of the cave. The birch trees blocked the view at first, but once they were out of the grove Nikki stopped, her eyes wide. They were at the bottom of a valley shaped like a deep box. The sides of the valley went straight up more than a mile, to end at craggy peaks covered in snow and ice. A river cut through the middle of the valley, its source a huge waterfall as tall as a ten-story building. Nikki gulped as she watched the water crashing down from the top of the falls into the boiling pool below. She turned quickly away, not wanting to remember her moments of panic when the crushing columns of water pummeled her deeper and deeper into the pool.

She hurried after the man. He was walking through a grassy meadow dotted with tiny yellow flowers. Despite being nervous about meeting the Headman Nikki found the valley extremely beautiful. Hawks soared up in the blue air above the mountain peaks and little ground squirrels poked their heads out of their burrows as she passed.

The meadow flowed to the river's edge and the man continued along a path following the rushing water. This wasn't a tame river. It had no boat traffic. This was a powerful mountain river whose deep green water fell over rapids which whipped the water into white sprays of mist and foam.

Nikki took deep breaths of the clean mountain air as she walked and soon began to feel better. As her lungs and her mind cleared she began to have misgivings about all the beauty around her. The valley wasn't large. Maybe a few miles wide and a bit farther in length. She could see from one end to the other, and as far as she could tell there was no way out. The mountains were sheer granite cliffs on all sides except one. And in that direction a huge cloud of mist rose into the sky. Nikki suspected that the river poured over another waterfall there. And judging by the amount of water vapor it was sending into the air it was even bigger than the one she'd fallen over. So her options for getting out of the valley were to go over another waterfall or to climb cliffs that were completely vertical. That left the Long Stairs that the man had mentioned, but she was pretty sure there would be a guard on those. The people in this valley didn't seem like the welcoming kind. They probably had guards everywhere. They seemed to be hiding down here for some reason.

"We cross here," said the man, pointing to a row of boulders which jutted out of the rapids.

Nikki felt her knees begin to shake as she watched the man jump from boulder to boulder. One slip and the rapids would carry him downstream toward the waterfall at the end of the valley. They were closer to it now and the cloud of mist it generated rose far into the sky.

When the man reached the other side of the river he waved impatiently for her to join him. Nikki wondered what would happen if she turned and ran back to the cave. The entrance to the Long Stairs might be somewhere nearby. Maybe she could slip past the guards. But even if she managed to climb the stairs and find another boat she would still face the problem of the underground river. Its current was too strong for her to row against. She'd just go over the falls again.

That decided it. She stepped gingerly onto the first boulder, trying to ignore the sound of the rapids roaring all around her. The top of the rock was wet, but not as slippery as she'd feared. It was rough and pitted and her Nikes gripped the surface well. She managed pretty well until the middle of the river. The gap between the boulders was widest there and her legs were a lot shorter than the man's. She hesitated, half crouching on a boulder.

"Just jump!" shouted the man. "The distance is not as far as your fear is making it."

Nikki wasn't so sure about that. She was afraid, certainly, but she was also pretty good at judging distances. She estimated that the gap to the next boulder was about five feet. Without a running start it was a long way for her to jump. The man had gone across the rocks at a run, leaping from boulder to boulder and using his momentum to make his leaps easier. She was stuck with a standing start.

You can't stay on this rock forever, she told herself. Your legs will get colder and weaker the longer you wait. She took a deep breath, crouched down even lower, and threw herself at the next boulder. Her legs didn't make it but her upper half did. She belly-flopped onto the rock, hugging it tightly with both arms. Her feet scrabbled for a foothold and she pulled herself up on top of the rock. Her ribs ached from their collision with the rock but there was no time to assess the damage.

"Hurry up!" yelled the man. "Daylight is fading and we still have to climb the Eagle Stairs. It is not wise to climb them after dark. Men far more sure-footed than you have fallen to their deaths in the attempt."

Nikki ignored him, especially the part about people falling to their deaths. She had enough things to worry about. She stood up to study the rest of the path across the boulders. To her relief the worst was over. The rest of the rocks were spaced close together, not more than a foot apart. She darted over them, anxious to be on solid ground once more. When she reached the riverbank she collapsed onto her knees, her hands grasping the sandy soil.

"No time to rest," said the man, grabbing her arm and yanking her none too gently to her feet. "It's not just fading daylight that we're racing. The Headman locks out anyone who hasn't reached the Sanctuary by nightfall. And I don't fancy spending the night in the guard shack outside the main gates. You get cold straw to sleep on and the leftovers of the kitchen."

He led her through meadows turning gray with the fading of the light. Up on the peaks of the mountains the sun still shone in a blue sky, but down in the valley the cliffs cast huge shadows which brought an early sunset.

After an hour of walking they reached the far end of the valley. Nikki could feel the ground vibrate with the tremendous power of the waterfall they were approaching. Huge clouds of mist hung in the air. The cliffs on both sides closed in on the river. There was no way forward except over the falls.

Nikki wondered if there was another underground stairway they were going to go down. She tilted her head back, looking up at the cliffs for a cave or tunnel. Then she saw it. Perched half a mile above her head, clinging to the sheer granite cliffs just below the snow-line, was a cluster of stone buildings. Their walls were massively thick and their roofs were shingled with gray slate. Hawks circled the buildings and ravens perched on its rooftops.

"This way," said the man. "Step where I step. There are broken places where it's easy to stumble."

He suddenly seemed to disappear right into the mountain side, but when Nikki followed she saw that he was climbing steep stone stairs. They were cut into a gash in the cliff, invisible to anyone on the valley floor.

The stairs switchbacked up the mountain side, occasionally going through short tunnels but mostly open to the air. Each step was uncomfortably high, straining the legs, and they were worn smooth from long years of erosion and rain. Falling rocks had crashed onto them, reducing some steps to rubble. Nikki was soon out of breath as she struggled to keep up with the man. She concentrated on watching his feet. He deftly dodged the steps which were broken and cracked.

As they rounded a switchback the rock wall which had enclosed the stairs on the valley side suddenly ended. To her horror Nikki found herself climbing a staircase which had nothing but empty air on one side. The drop to the valley floor was hundreds of feet below.

"They'll kill you if you turn back," said the man, looking over his shoulder at her.

He seemed to be reading her thoughts. Nikki had just decided to go back and take her chances with the Long Stairs and the underground river. It seemed like a better option than falling hundreds of feet to her death.

"We don't allow strangers to wander freely in our valley," said the man. "All intruders are brought before the Headman. I can't allow you to go back. I am bound by our laws to bring you to the Sanctuary."

Nikki glared up at him, but he just turned away and continued climbing. He was right, thought Nikki grumpily. There wasn't really anything else she could do but to keep following him. He could catch her easily if she tried to make a run for it back down the stairs. She was a fast runner and quite agile, but she was no match for someone who had probably gone up and down these stairs for years. Most likely she'd just fall and break her neck. She gritted her teeth and forced her sore legs to keep climbing. She found it wasn't too bad as long as she kept her eyes on her feet and never looked over the edge.

The full moon had just cleared the mountain tops when they finally reached the Sanctuary. The last rays of the setting sun stained the snowy peaks blood red. Nikki stopped to catch her breath and rub her aching legs as she warily eyed the courtyard the stairs had led them to. Rough stone slabs covered the ground and the courtyard walls were chiseled straight out of the mountain side. It was empty except for a well in the middle with a bucket hanging from a pulley. The bucket swung in the evening breeze, its creaking echoing off the rocks walls like the cry of a bat trying to find its prey. There was no decoration anywhere. No statues, no murals, no flowers or trees, no signs of daily life.

Nikki assumed that the building which formed the far side of the square was the Sanctuary. It was two stories high with walls of grey stone ten feet thick. She could see the head of a guard as he walked along the top of the wall on patrol. The only entrance seemed to be the main gate. It was a massive wooden structure bolted to the stone walls with iron hinges as thick as her arm. Just outside the gate, built against the wall of the Sanctuary, Nikki spotted the guard house the man had mentioned. It was a shabby wooden hut with an angry looking mastiff chained up out front. The dog sprang to its feet as they approached and began barking wildly. It strained at its chain, looking eager to tear them apart.

The man ignored the mastiff and hurried up to the gate. He banged on it three times with his fist and a smaller door which was cut into the huge gate creaked open. He disappeared through the door without looking back.

Nikki stood uncertainly in the middle of the courtyard. Maybe this was her chance to make a run for it. The man who had brought her there seemed to consider his job finished, and no one else appeared in the doorway to the Sanctuary. She had just taken a step backward when she noticed that the guard on top of the wall was staring at her. He pulled an arrow from a quiver, notched it into a bow and took aim at her. Another guard suddenly appeared at the door of the guard house. Nikki took the hint and made a dash for the Sanctuary door, nearly tripping over the threshold in her hurry.

The outer wall of the Sanctuary was so thick that it formed a short tunnel. When Nikki emerged she found herself in another courtyard. In its center rose a pagoda-like building with stone layers stacked like a wedding cake. The man who had brought her was just entering a door on the bottom layer.

Nikki followed him into the building. The center of the structure was an empty core which rose straight up for five stories. A wooden staircase painted a dark red wound around and around the core. Nikki followed the man up the spiraling stairs. At least these stairs had guard rails on either side, but they creaked and swayed alarmingly. She noticed that the bolts which anchored the stairs to the rock walls of the building had come loose in many places. The people who lived in the Sanctuary didn't seem to maintain it very well.

At the top of the stairs were two guards flanking an open door. Nikki's guide ignored them and passed through. When Nikki followed she saw what looked like the throne room of a very poor kingdom. Against one wall a crudely carved wooden chair sat on a raised platform. Iron candlesticks taller than her head were placed in a semi-circle around the chair. Fat yellow candles gave off a foul-smelling smoke. Wooden panels painted a deep dark red covered the walls from floor to ceiling. Scorch marks blackened the flagstone floor. There were no windows. The only light came from a firepit in the center of the room. Thirty or forty men dressed in ragged tunics and trousers were seated on mats scattered across the floor. The room smelled of unwashed armpits.

At first Nikki thought the room was bare of decoration, but as her eyes adjusted to the dim light she saw a portrait painted on one panel. She blinked at it in surprise. There was no mistaking those glaring eyes and bushy, menacing eyebrows. The portrait even captured the sheen of his purple silk robe. It was Maleficious.

"You seem familiar with our benefactor," said a voice to her left.

Nikki turned as a man rose from one of the mats on the floor and approached her. He wasn't a particularly tall man, he didn't carry any weapons, and the only disturbing thing about him was the empty socket where his left eye used to be, yet Nikki immediately felt both fear and dislike. It was his voice, she thought. It was cold with hostility. The man who had brought her to the Sanctuary had seemed indifferent to her, but this man almost seemed to hate her even though they'd never met.

"Um," she said, glancing at the portrait. "I, uh, had the pleasure of meeting him once. At Castle Cogent."

A murmur went around the room at this, but the Headman, as Nikki had no doubt that he was, held up a hand and the room went quiet at once.

"You've met Maleficious," said the Headman. "I find this hard to believe. Why would such a great man, second in power only to the King, meet with a child?"

"Well, um, when you put it like that, no, it wasn't like he arranged a meeting with me. He just happened to be in the rose garden of Castle Cogent when Fuzz and Athena introduced me to the King."

There was an even louder outcry from the men in the room, though Nikki didn't understand why. She hadn't said anything the least bit insulting about Maleficious.

The Headman waved for silence again. "Fuzz and Athena. We know those names here. They are messengers of the King. And they are imps."

"Yes," said Nikki, looking at the Headman's face in alarm. It was turning an ugly shade of red. The veins in his empty eye socket bulged.

"Imps." The Headman spat on the floor. "Vermin. Why were you associating with vermin?"

Nikki just stared at him in shock. The hatred in his face was turning it into an inhuman mask. He looked completely deranged. She realized she had to think of some way to calm the situation, but her mind was completely blank. She knew there were pockets of prejudice in the Realm against the imps, but she had never encountered anything this extreme.

The Headman suddenly gestured to a man seated nearby. He jumped up and grabbed Nikki by the hair, forcing her head back.

The knife which appeared in the Headman's hand shone in the firelight. Nikki stared at it, mesmerized, like a mouse about to be eaten by a cat.

"Start talking, girl," said the Headman, "or I'll slit your throat and throw your body off the mountainside. Our custom is to let children who wander into our valley go free, but no one who associates with imp vermin leaves here alive."

"I wasn't associating with them," gasped Nikki, frantically trying to come up with a believable story. For some reason Kira popped into her mind. Kira and her brother were originally from the Southern Isles. They had an accent different from the other people she'd met in the Realm. Maybe the Southern Isles could explain her own accent. "I got separated from my parents while we were touring Castle Cogent. My parents are traders from the Southern Isles. They were bringing a shipment of silks to the castle for the King and his nobles. As you said, the imps are just the King's messengers. They were just presenting me to the King. I'd never seen them before. Or since." Nikki knew she wasn't the world's greatest liar. When she lied her face tended to flush from embarrassment. Fortunately at that moment her face was pointed at the ceiling.

The silence in the room seemed to last forever, but finally Nikki heard the Headman snap his fingers. The man holding her hair released her.

Nikki fought the urge to run. The Headman was like a wild animal, a bear or a mountain lion. The rule of survival was to never run if you met such a creature. It triggered their hunting instincts and you became prey. She had no desire to become a dead rabbit speared by the Headman's knife.

The Headman stared at her for a long moment, then finally put his knife back into the sheath on his belt. "If your parents are at Castle Cogent then what are you doing in the Mystic Mountains? We are a long way from the comforts of the King's court. We have no need of silks from the Southern Isles here."

A long stream of images from her travels around the Realm crossed Nikki's mind, but she couldn't come up with a good story about why she was alone in the mountains. Most of her travels involved the imps, and she wasn't going to go near that topic again. What she needed was a distraction. Something which would make the Headman and his followers forget all about her. And she knew just the thing. From the way the Headman had talked about Maleficious it seemed that he didn't know the King's advisor was dead.

Nikki walked shakily over to the portrait on the wall, giving the men seated on the floor a wide berth. She stared up at the painting for a moment, as if she was a student visiting an art museum. "It's very good," she said. "It looks just like him. How soon before his death was it painted?"

There was a stunned silence behind her, as she'd known there would be. She just hoped that they weren't so shocked by the news that they'd decide to kill the messenger.

"Maleficious is dead?"

It wasn't the Headman who spoke but the man who'd brought her across the valley.

Nikki turned to him and nodded. "Yes. He was killed several weeks ago. Murdered."

The men started to whisper furiously among themselves.

The Headman walked slowly to the raised dais and sat down in the throne-like chair. "Who killed him?" he asked, his voice as harsh as if it had been dipped in acid.

"Rufius," said Nikki.

"Who?" asked the Headman.

Nikki stared at him in surprise. It had never occurred to her that they wouldn't have heard of Rufius, assistant to Maleficious, advisor to the King, and rapidly becoming one of the most powerful people in the Realm. But as she thought about it she realized that it made sense. Rufius's rise to power had happened very rapidly, beginning only a few months ago, not long after she'd come to the Realm of Reason. And these men in their remote valley in the Mystic Mountains were very isolated. Cut off from the rest of the Realm. It would take news from the King's court a long time to reach them.

"Rufius was an assistant to Maleficious," she finally said. "But then he took over more and more of Maleficious's duties and became a trusted advisor to the King."

"What does this worthless piece of toad vomit, this Rufius, look like?" asked the Headman.

"Well, he's a very young man. About twenty-five I'd say. He's medium height, very pale, with curly black hair. He always wears a spotlessly clean black tunic. And sandals."

"And where is he now?" asked the Headman, the vein in his empty eye socket bulging.

"Deceptionville," said Nikki at once. She had no problem at all pointing these strange valley-dwellers in Rufius's direction. They looked like they could give him all kinds of trouble, and he deserved as much trouble as she could throw at him.

The Headman looked at her intently. "And why would he murder

Maleficious, the wisest advisor to the King this Realm has ever seen?"

Nikki shrugged. "Power, of course. Rufius wants power and lots of it. Maleficious was an old man who was in his way."

Angry shouts came from the men seated on the floor. A few of them jumped to their feet.

"That's what Rufius called him," said Nikki quickly. "No one else called him that, of course. He was greatly respected by everyone in the Realm." She could feel her face flush at that whopper of a lie, but fortunately the Headman was no longer staring at her. He rose from his chair and walked over to the portrait of Maleficious.

"He gave us this valley long ago, in my grandfather's time," said the Headman, more to himself than to his men. "He was my grandfather's brother. He gave us this Sanctuary, built many centuries ago by forgotten ancestors. Gave it to us to live in when the King's grandfather rejected our help and tried to banish us from the Realm. To banish us for treason. For trying to defend our land against vermin like the imps." He spat on the floor. "It is the monarch who now sits on the throne at Castle Cogent who is treasonous. He consorts with imps, listens to their lies, lets them travel freely about the Realm, gives them land and jobs which should go to their betters."

He whipped his knife out of its sheath and held it above his head. "We will hunt down this Rufius, this sniveling dog who has killed our mighty benefactor. We will hunt him from one end of the Realm to the other. He shall meet his doom at our hands. And then, well we shall see. We have been patient, here in our Sanctuary, but I say now is the time to take our rightful place in the Realm. Now is the time to remove our treasonous King from his throne, and to drive every imp from our lands."

His men cheered loudly and jumped to their feet. They followed the Headman as he stalked from the room.

Nikki found herself alone in the fire-lit room, listening to the pounding of their boots as they rushed down the spiral staircase. She stared for a long moment at the portrait of Maleficious, wondering what it was she had just unleashed. She'd wanted to point the men at Rufius, not at the King. She tried not to think about what might happen if the Headman decided to go the King's court at Castle Cogent. The castle was well-guarded, but she wondered if Rufius had managed to corrupt the loyalty of the castle guards the way he had corrupted the Knights of the Iron Fist.

Nikki rubbed her forehead in frustration, but there wasn't much she could do about the situation. The best thing she could do was to meet back up with Fuzz and Athena in Kingston. They'd be able to warn the King. She sighed and left the empty room. The two guards who had flanked the door were gone. She peered over the railing of the spiral staircase. No one was in sight, but she could hear voices shouting in the courtyard five stories below. She crept down the stairs, expecting to be stopped at any moment, but the building was completely empty. As was the inner courtyard of the Sanctuary. She could hear men shouting orders in the outer courtyard where the guard house was. She passed through the tunnel in the thick outer wall and froze in astonishment.

Hundreds of men were assembled in the courtyard. Some were unwinding ropes, some were running into the guard house and coming out with long rolls of linen which reminded Nikki of furled sails. Others were manning a huge charcoal brazier which had been setup near the well. The coals in the brazier were so red-hot they looked like tiny burning suns. As she watched the men unrolled the huge rolls of cloth on the ground and fastened iron buckets to one end. Then they tied huge wicker baskets below the iron buckets. The baskets were big enough to hold twenty people, and Nikki suddenly guessed what it was the men were doing. Her guess was confirmed when the men began shoveling red-hot coals from the brazier into each iron bucket. The linen tied to each bucket began to billow and flap and lift off the ground. The cloths were sewn shut at one end and as the hot air from the coals entered they expanded like a balloon. Which is exactly what they were. Hot air balloons.

A group of twenty men got into one of the wicker baskets and shoveled more coals into their iron bucket. The balloon over their head expanded into a fat round ball fifty feet in diameter and the basket full of men began to rise slowly into the air. It rose higher and higher, just clearing the top of the pagoda building in the inner courtyard. Then the wind caught it and pushed it in the direction of the waterfall at the end of the valley.

So this was how they got out of the valley, thought Nikki. She stood transfixed as balloon after balloon took off. It was only after the last one had disappeared over the horizon that she realized how quiet it was. Every single man had left.

Then she heard a low growl and realized she wasn't completely alone. The giant mastiff was still pulling at its chain in front of the guard house. She stood staring at it for a long moment. It was very clear the dog wasn't in the mood to become friends. She wondered if the men planned to come back. As mean as the animal looked, she couldn't just leave it there to starve.

The guards probably fed it, she thought, glancing at the door to the guard house. The dog's chain didn't quite extend to the guard house door. She slowly walked toward it, the dog barking furiously. It lunged at her but its chain brought it up short several feet from her. She poked her head into the guard house. Sure enough, a pile of meat scraps and bones lay in a big wooden bowl. There was also a tin dish which was probably the dog's water bowl. As she picked this up she noticed a stack of cloth in one corner. And a pile of iron buckets.

She began to shake her head vigorously. No, she couldn't. She'd crash. She'd fall to her death. With shaking hands she took the tin dish out to the well and filled it, pushing it within reach of the dog using a broom she found leaning against the guard house wall. She pushed the bowl of meat scraps to the animal in the same way and then stood leaning on the broom. She could smell the smoke still drifting up from the brazier.

Taking the broom with her to support her shaky legs, she reluctantly walked over to the brazier and peeked inside. A mound of coals was still glowing red-hot down in the bottom.

"Oh, just do it," she muttered to herself. "There's no point in wasting time thinking about it. The coals will just burn out. And then the only way out of this blasted valley will be the Long Stairs. I'll just end up going over the waterfall again, and this time there won't be anyone around to fish me out."

She sighed and dropped the broom. This time when she entered the guard house the dog ignored her. It was too busy scarfing up scraps of meat and crunching bones. She picked through the pile of linen, trying to find a balloon which was smaller than the rest. She wouldn't need as much lift for her balloon as one which had to lift twenty men. She dragged out a likely candidate and spread it out on the ground near the brazier. She went back for ropes and an iron bucket and managed to tie these to the linen balloon in a similar fashion to what the men had done. She gave her knots an extra yank to make sure they were tight and then headed to the pile of wicker baskets the men had left stacked against the wall. Here she met her first obstacle. The huge baskets were stacked inside each other like soup bowls and she couldn't budge them. She tried hanging all her weight off the side of the top basket, hoping to tip the whole pile over so she could unstick the baskets from each other, but it was no use. The pile was much heavier than she was.

Nikki wiped the sweat off her forehead and eyed the pile of baskets. Maybe she could just drag her linen balloon over and attach it to the whole pile. A glance up at the Sanctuary walls squashed that idea. The outer wall where the baskets were piled was right up against the mountainside. Her balloon would crash right into it. And anyway, the small mound of coals left in the brazier might have trouble generating enough hot air to lift five heavy baskets.

She gave up on the baskets and returned to the guard house. All she needed was something to sit in. There was a rough wooden table inside, with four hefty chairs. Nikki sat in one and tried to imagine floating over the mountains in it. Nope. She needed something which would protect her from the wind and from any close calls with tree tops or mountain crags. She got up and rummaged in a pile of odds and ends in one corner. She found a wooden box full of old clothing, but when she tried to pull it into the center of the room a slat broke off. She shuddered, imaging the bottom falling out of the box when she was hundreds of feet in the air. Then she spotted a large grayish metal object. She dragged it out of the corner. It was a tin washtub, probably used by the men for washing clothes or even bathing in. She climbed in. There was plenty of room for her to sit in and it looked sturdy enough to hold her weight. She dragged the tub out to the balloon and fastened it to the ropes by its metal handles.

The moment to leave had arrived. Nikki forced herself to rush back and forth to the brazier, shoveling hot coals into her iron bucket. If she stopped to rest for a moment she knew she'd chicken out. Better to just get on with it as quickly as possible.

Her balloon soon inflated. It was already lifting the tin washtub a few inches off the ground. A few more shovelfuls should do it. Nikki looked over her shoulder at the dog. It was peacefully gnawing at a bone. She quietly snuck over to where the dog's chain was anchored to an iron spike in the ground. The dog ignored her while she dug up the spike. The animal didn't even notice that it was now free to roam wherever it liked.

A last few shovelfuls of coal inflated the balloon to its full size. The washtub suddenly lifted off the ground and Nikki climbed in just in time. The tub swayed alarmingly as she climbed in, but she found that if she stayed completely still it leveled out. The balloon rose straight up just as the men's balloons had done, then it was caught by the wind and pushed over the inner courtyard, just clearing the top of the pagoda building.

Nikki gritted her teeth and scrunched her eyes shut as the balloon passed over the edge of the Sanctuary. Now there was nothing below her but the valley floor, thousands of feet down.

She didn't open her eyes again until she felt the mist and heard the roaring of the waterfall. It generated such dense clouds of mist that she couldn't really see it. Its waters filled the valley from side to side and the sound they made filled her ears. She kept a wary eye on the rocky cliffs bordering the river, but her balloon floated straight over the middle of the waterfall as if it was a train on a track. The winds in the valley must be extremely constant, she thought. Always blowing in the same direction. That was why the men were able to use the balloons as a reliable means of transportation. Because you couldn't steer a hot air balloon. It just went wherever the wind blew it.

When she was past the mist she noticed that the balloon was no longer following the river. Below her now were endless miles of thick forest. She turned to look behind her, causing the washtub to tilt. Nikki let out a shriek and closed her eyes, freezing like a statue until the tub stopped rocking.

Once her heart had stopped beating wildly she slowly opened her eyes and carefully turned her head. She had left the Mystic Mountains behind. She was on the other side of the mighty range, their snowy crags glowing red in the last rays of the setting sun. Nikki faced forward again, feeling the sun on her back. If the sun was behind her then she must be travelling east. That was fortunate, as long as the winds kept her on this course. The sea coast was to the east, and the coast was where she wanted to go. She doubted the winds would drop her right at Kingston, even if her coals lasted that long, but anywhere along the coast was a big improvement over being lost in the Mystic Mountains.

She glanced up at the iron bucket above her head. It was amazing that she could travel along using nothing but hot air. The heat from the coals caused the air inside the balloon to expand, becoming less dense than the surrounding air. The lighter air inside the balloon floated on the heavier air around it the same way a leaf floats on a pool of water. And so the balloon was lifted up. The floating of a less dense substance on a heavier substance was called a displacement force or a buoyant force. In her world the Chinese and the Thai people had used this principle for centuries to send lanterns into the air during festivals. And in the eighteenth century the Montgolfier brothers in France had used the same principle to make the first manned hot-air balloon. The displacement force was related to the ideal gas law. In her AP Physics class her teacher had launched a small lantern powered by a candle to illustrate the ideal gas law, $PV=nRT$. The ideal gas law showed the relationships between pressure, volume, and temperature of a gas. Her teacher had gotten yelled at by the vice principal when the lantern had landed on a student's head and set his hair on fire, but the student wasn't hurt and the lantern incident had burned the ideal gas law into Nikki's brain in a way no amount of studying ever would have.

The heat from the bucket was very welcome in the chilly evening air, but Nikki wondered how long it would last. The coals would eventually burn out and the balloon would descend back to earth. She scanned the horizon but could see nothing but trees. Nothing but pines and firs with the occasional rocky outcropping sticking up into the sky. She was pretty sure she was looking at the Trackless Forest, the immense and uninhabited forest where she and Curio had gotten lost. Her stomach growled as she remembered how hungry they'd been until they'd stumbled at last out of the forest and into the camp of Griff and her crew.

There were only two groups of people who lived in the Trackless Forest, as far as she knew. The monks whose encampment Athena had led them to deep in the forest. And the imps whose headquarters was on the edge of the forest near the Haunted Hills, where they'd spent one night and nearly been captured by the Knights of the Iron Fist. Of the two Nikki much preferred the imp headquarters. The monks had been friendly to her at first, but her encounter with them had not ended well when she'd questioned some of their ideas. They were just a little too fanatical for her taste and she doubted she'd get a friendly welcome if Athena wasn't with her.

But there seemed to be little chance of finding either group. The Trackless Forest was just too immense. The best she could hope for was that her supply of coal would last all the way to the coast. Or at least within sight of it. If she spotted the ocean before the balloon descended to the ground she could probably walk the rest of the way to the coast if she kept to a straight line. She sighed, wishing Athena was with her. Athena had wonderful tracking skills. She could navigate using the stars. Nikki looked up at the first faint stars shining in the evening sky. She couldn't spot any familiar constellations, not even the big dipper or Orion. Not that they would have done her much good. She didn't have any idea how to navigate by the stars. Kira had tried to teach her using a sextant on board Griff's ship, but she didn't remember exactly how it was done, and besides, she had no sextant. She closed her eyes, took a deep breath, and tried to summon up as much calmness and patience as she could. Calmness and patience were admittedly in short supply when you were floating in a tin washtub hundreds of feet in the air, but she did her best.

Chapter Five

Anchors Away

NIKKI CAREFULLY PRIED one hand off the rim of the washtub. Her fingers were nearly frozen from clutching the rim for hours and hours. She squinted down at the dark treetops below. Was it just her imagination, or were the trees closer than before? The moon had set and it was nearly pitch black. It was very hard to get her bearings in such complete darkness. She lifted her hand up to the iron bucket full of coals. Yes, she was pretty sure it was cooler than before. The balloon must be descending whether she could tell or not.

She closed her eyes and listened. She heard the wind rustling the tops of the trees and an occasional click, which was probably a bat hunting using echo location. As she concentrated on hearing instead of seeing a new sound gradually came to her notice. It was a roaring sound. At first she thought it was just the wind, but then she noticed that it had a rhythm to it, like waves crashing on a beach. Her eyes flew open. That's exactly what it was! She'd made it to the coast.

The line of white on the horizon gradually came closer and closer. Soon she could smell the sea air and hear the squawk of seagulls. The whiteness resolved into breakers crashing onto a sandy shore. The wind her balloon was riding was pushing it right towards the ocean.

Nikki's relief at reaching the coast soon turned to alarm, however. She could see a little better now due to the light reflecting off the crashing waves. It showed that she was still very high in the air. Too high to jump out. In a regular hot-air balloon she would have just turned down the gas to bring the balloon back to earth. She glanced up at the bucket of coals above her head. She had no way to cool them down. She wasn't going to stick her hand in hot coals and scoop them out. She should have brought the shovel from the Sanctuary with her, but it was too late now.

She watched helplessly as the balloon floated over the beach and out to sea. She would have to jump, she thought reluctantly. But not quite yet. True, the water would break her fall, but even a watery landing wouldn't help from this height. She'd have to wait. Fortunately the wind had slowed and the balloon wasn't speeding out to sea. She looked back at the waves crashing on the beach, wondering how far she could swim. She'd gone to summer camp one year on Lake Monona in Madison, Wisconsin. Her bunk mates had dared her to swim across the lake. She'd made it, but just barely, and she'd had to rest a lot by floating on her back. Lake Monona was three miles across and she'd been on her very last ounce of energy by the time she reached the other shore. So three miles was probably her maximum swimming distance. Though the lake was a lot warmer than the ocean, and it didn't have waves.

As she anxiously watched the shoreline getting farther and farther away she felt a warmth on her back. The sun was just starting to rise. The ocean below her began to sparkle in the sunlight. She cautiously leaned forward to glance over the rim of the washtub. The surface of the water was definitely closer now. Nikki guessed the height was about one hundred feet. Still too high. Another thirty feet lower and then she'd jump. She was trying to mentally prepare herself for the jump when she gasped.

There was a ship below her. A three-masted ship with square sails. It was sailing with the wind behind it and it was headed straight for her.

Her first thought was that the Knights of the Iron Fist had found her. But that seemed impossible. There was no way they could have tracked her. Then as she peered down at the ship she noticed that some of the people on the deck were shouting at her. One of them was looking at her through a telescope. As the ship drew closer she suddenly realized that the telescope-holder was Kira. Nikki could see her blue-ribboned dreadlocks flying in the wind. It was Griff's ship!

She could hear them now. They were shouting something about ducks and they were making hand signals at her. Ducks? What the heck? Then she noticed Kira's brother Krill standing in the bow. He was putting what looked like a harpoon onto his shoulder.

Not ducks. Duck! Nikki ducked below the rim of the washtub just as the harpoon shot from Krill's shoulder. There was a whistling noise as the harpoon tore right through the balloon and out the other side. Hot air rushed out of the balloon and it plummeted toward the water.

The washtub tilted violently. Nikki grabbed hold of a rope as hot coals from the bucket above her head rained down on her. She dangled from the rope until she was ten feet from the water. As she took a deep breath and let go she heard the washtub hit the surface with a giant splash. She held her breath and swam blindly underwater until she was away from the tangling ropes and fabric of the balloon. When she surfaced and wiped the water out of her eyes she saw the ship looming above her. It looked huge from that angle, with barnacles covering its mighty hull just above the water line. It had furled its sails and was floating gently on the waves.

"Ahoy there!" called Griff, the ship's captain, grinning down at her. "Would you perchance be in need of a ride into port?"

"Yes please," Nikki shouted.

Krill threw a rope ladder over the side and Nikki swam up to it. It wasn't easy climbing up the heaving side of a ship. The rope ladder didn't quite reach the water, so she had to stretch for the lowest rung and then pull herself up using only her arms for the first couple of feet.

But after banging her knuckles many times and her nose once she managed to reach the top. Krill grabbed her under the armpits and hauled her over the railing.

Kira rushed up and enfolded Nikki in a hug.

"Don't" said Nikki. "I'm soaking wet." She brushed a piece of seaweed off of Kira's deer-hide tunic.

Kira just laughed. "Somebody's always soaking wet on this ship. If anyone gets too smelly we just throw them over the side. Saves time doing laundry."

Griff stomped up in her heavy leather boots, long black coat and three-cornered hat. She patted Nikki on the back. "Good to see you again, young lady." The captain's bright blue eyes twinkled in her deeply tanned face. "And here's someone who *you'll* be glad to see again."

"Hello, Miss." Curio ran forward, hopping up and down in excitement.

"Curio!" Nikki pulled the little boy into a hug, noticing that his messy blonde hair now came up to her chin. "Why, I think you've actually grown since I saw you last. And it's only been what? Two weeks?"

"I have Miss. I have. I'm taller than Tarn now." He pointed at a scowling imp with a long grey beard who was sitting on a barrel darning a fishing net. Scratch, the ship's mangy, one-eyed cat was watching the rhythmic movements of the darning needle in fascination.

"Not much of an accomplishment," growled Tarn. "I'm short even for an imp, but I can still lick you in a fistfight, you toothless little codfish. And don't you forget it."

Curio just laughed and made a rude whistling sound through his two missing front teeth.

"Are Athena and Fuzz on board?" asked Nikki. "I really need to talk to them."

Griff shook her head. "Afraid not. They're holed up in the mansion of the Prince of Physics. Plotting something." She sighed. "I just hope they're careful. Things are bad right now in Kingston and getting worse by the day. That conniving scoundrel Rufius is making everyone swear an oath of loyalty to him. Says he's doing it in the name of the King, but everyone knows Rufius is close to kicking the King off the throne and taking it for himself."

Nikki had urgent things to report about Rufius's activities in Deceptionville. Not to mention Fortuna's deadly potions and the crazy men from the Mystic Mountains who wanted revenge for the death of Maleficious. But she wasn't going to get into all that on the deck of Griff's ship. Athena and Fuzz knew way more about the Realm than she did and they might want to keep some of her information from becoming public. She leaned over the rail and watched the remains of her balloon sink into the sea.

"How did you find me?" she asked. "I could have sworn no one knew where I was."

"We didn't find you," said Griff. "It was pure luck. We were tracking a school of cod when Kira spotted your flying contraption in her telescope. Bit surprised, we were. We've seen similar flying orbs in the Southern Isles, but those are a lot smaller. They use them in rituals and celebrations. This is the first time I've seen one big enough to carry a person. Now, speaking of cod, we need to get back to business. Cod is going for a high price right now in Kingston. There are food shortages since Rufius decided to quarter the Knights of the Iron Fist in Kingston's tournament grounds. Those metal-headed idiots eat like a swarm of locusts. Tarn, get off that barrel and up into the crow's nest. See if you can spot that school again. Krill, take the helm."

"Come on," said Kira. "Let's go down below. I have some dry clothes you can borrow."

"When you're ready, Miss, I'll cook you up a nice flapjack," said Curio. "I've been helping Posie with all the cooking. So far what I've cooked is hardtack and flapjacks, and none of the crew have gotten stomach churnings. Though I did set a sail on fire. But Krill put it out right away, so no harm done. Though Tarn did say he was gonna throw me over the side, but that's just his way of talking. Krill says Tarn is all beard and no action and that I should just ignore anything he says. Krill lets me help with all his chores . . ."

"Speaking of chores," said Kira, "why don't you go help Krill at the helm? You can check the compass for him."

"Right away Miss." Curio saluted smartly and dashed off.

Kira laughed. "That kid has more energy than a hummingbird. I just wish he had as much sense as he has energy. That sail wasn't the only thing he's set on fire. He was boiling water for tea when he set Griff's favorite coat on fire. Fortunately she wasn't wearing it at the time."

"He's a good kid," said Nikki. "He means well."

"Oh, I know," said Kira. "I think he just needs a parent to look after him. Griff actually offered to make him a permanent crew member, but he declined her offer. Said another lady had already promised him a home."

Nikki nodded. "Gwen. You haven't met her. She's the daughter of Lady Ursula of Muddled Manor."

"Oh my," said Kira. "What fancy friends you do have!"

Nikki gave her a friendly swat on the arm. "Knock it off and show me where the dry clothes are. I'm freezing."

Kira led her down into the hold of the ship. They passed Griff's cabin and the large open space where hammocks for the crew were swinging from the ceiling. Loud snores came from the tiny cabin which belonged to Posie, the ship's cook.

"Posie's sleeping a lot lately," said Kira with a worried tone. "Griff says she's getting too old for a sea-faring life, but Posie won't hear of settling down in Kingston. Griff took her to see a nice little cottage not far from the mansion of the Prince of Physics, but Posie just stuck her nose in the air and said it smelled like land-lubbers."

Kira continued down a narrow staircase that wound deep into the ship's hull. "My cabin's down here. It's a pain being so far down, but at least it's private. Krill has to sleep in the crew quarters in a hammock. He's used to it now, but for our first month onboard he used to spend every night vomiting. Those hammocks swing like pendulums when we're at sea."

There was a sudden splash and Kira swore.

"What's the matter?" asked Nikki, a few steps behind.

"Water in the hold," said Kira crossly. "The bilge pump must be stuck again." She led the way through ankle-deep water that soon became knee-deep. They passed an open door and Kira gestured impatiently. "My cabin," she said. "After we fix the pump we'll have to get you some dry clothes from Griff's cabin. My clothes chest is underwater."

Kira led the way down to the very bottom of the hold. The water was now waist-deep.

It wasn't as dark as Nikki had expected. Tiny rays of light came in through small chinks in the thick timbers of the hull far above their heads.

Kira waved her hand vaguely at the light rays. "The crew was supposed to put another coat of tar on the hull the last time we were in port, to patch those holes, but there's such a high demand for fish right now that we set sail again immediately after our last catch." She shoved aside a wooden box labelled "Tea" which had floated into her path. "There's always leaking in any ship, but usually our pump can keep up with it. It was built by the Prince of Physics himself and it's one of the best in the Realm. The Prince does a lot for us. He gave me that sextant I showed you the last time you were here. I think I mentioned that he's a distant relative of Griff's. It's handy to have friends in high places."

Kira waded over to a ledge sticking out of the side of the hull and climbed up onto it. Nikki climbed up after her.

"There's probably something stuck in the pump," said Kira, opening the top of a large wooden box which was fastened to the ledge. "Yep, seaweed." She pulled out a long strand of kelp and dropped it in the bilge water. "Be grateful it's just seaweed. Last time it was a pulverized octopus. The smell lasted for weeks."

Nikki stuck her hand in the box and helped Kira pull out another strand. Once they'd cleared out all the seaweed Nikki peered inside the box. It appeared to be a sort of suction pump. When she pushed on a flap which covered the top of the box she could see that beneath it there was a piston inside a wooden cylinder. A handle projected from the top of the box and into the cylinder. She guessed that when someone pushed down on the handle the piston was pushed down against the water, compressing it and forcing it up the sides of the piston into a long bronze pipe which ran from the box up to the top of the hull. Since the pipe was much smaller in diameter than the cylinder the water would be forced upward and expelled from the ship. It looked similar to force pumps which were still used on some farms in Wisconsin for irrigating crops.

Kira stuck her arm way down inside the cylinder. "I think we got it all." She put the lid back on the wooden box. "While we're here we may as well pump the water out. It's supposed to be Ralph's job. He's supposed to come down here and pump twice a day, but he's been busy repairing nets." She pointed at the pump handle. "Guests first," said with a grin.

Nikki grabbed the handle with both hands and pushed. Nothing happened.

Kira chuckled. "You have to put your weight on it."

Nikki nodded and leaned all her body weight on the handle. This time she could feel the piston very slowly and reluctantly slide down. Water gurgled up the bronze pipe and far overhead she could hear a stream of water splash into the ocean.

After ten pumps Nikki was exhausted. She leaned against the hull of the ship gasping for air.

Kira laughed and took over. She also had to throw her whole weight onto the handle. "This is why I usually let Ralph do this. He's a big strapping guy, a champion wrestler. He can push this down with one hand."

After taking turns again Kira waved Nikki to a stop. "That's enough for now. The water level's gone down by half. I'll ask Ralph to finish the job." She climbed down off the ledge. "Come on. We'll go up to Griff's cabin and borrow some of her clothes. She won't mind. They'll be a bit long for you, but that's better than being soaking wet."

Nikki felt quite swashbuckling when she joined the rest of the crew on deck. Kira had outfitted her in black trousers and a long black suede tunic belted at the waist with links of copper. Nikki also tried on a pair of Griff's boots, but they'd been too big for her so she kept her wet and ragged Nikes on. They didn't go with the rest of the outfit but they reminded her of home. She briefly wondered what her mother was doing at that moment, but brushed the thought aside when her eyes began to fill with tears. She twisted a stream of water out of her Westlake Debate Team T-shirt and hung it on her new copper belt. It had holes in the armpits and it reeked of sweat even after her swim in the ocean, but she couldn't bear to part with it.

She spent the rest of the day trying to stay out of the way as the crew chased down a school of codfish and hauled the fish up in huge nets. The catch was dumped into a hatch just behind the main mast. Any longing Nikki had ever had to be a pirate was dashed when the crew first opened the hatch. The smell of past catches that came wafting out was so disgusting that Nikki ran to the railing of the ship and vomited up the burnt pancakes that Curio had cooked for her.

As evening descended the last fish were hauled in and the hatch was closed, much to Nikki's relief. The ship changed course and headed back toward Kingston. It was fully dark with just a sliver of moon when she saw the torches of Kingston's harbor shining on the dark sea. Tall masts sprouted from the crowded docks like branchless trees. Much to her surprise the ship sailed right past the harbor.

"Where are we going?" she asked Curio, who was standing at the railing beside her.

"The Prince's dock," said Curio, looking like an odd misshapen lump in an old coat of Krill's which was much too big for him. Curio had rolled up several feet of hem and tucked the extra fabric into an old leather belt on the outside of the coat. In the dark it made him look like a tiny hunchbacked pregnant woman. "Our ship's been banned from docking in the main harbor. That dufus Rufius tried to get the King to ban Griff from Kingston completely, but the Prince stepped in and put a stop to that. So now we dock over there." He pointed to a long pier which came into view as they rounded a rocky headland. The turrets of the Southern Castle were just visible looming over the pier. "There's a secret tunnel which leads right from the dock up to the castle," Curio whispered. "I'm not supposed to know about it, but Krill told me and made me swear not to tell a soul. Course, he won't mind if I tell *you*. We're both hornorery members of the crew."

"I think you mean honorary members of the crew," said Nikki.

Curio nodded. "Right. Hornorery members."

The mainsail came down and the crew furled it on the mast. The ship glided slowly up to the dock and Krill jumped down onto it from the railing. Another crew member threw him a massive rope and he expertly tied the ship to a post.

A group of men with handcarts were gathered at the end of the pier. When the gangplank was dropped they trundled onto the ship with their carts and gathered on deck. The hatch was opened again and a huge wooden bucket was winched down into the hatch. The bucket came up overflowing with fish.

Nikki watched, glad that she was upwind of the hatch. The smell was blowing away from her. The winch the crew was using to unload the fish was a wooden frame with a large cylinder in the middle. As the crew turned handles on each side of the cylinder a rope wrapped around it to pull the bucket up. To lower it they turned the handles in the other direction, unwrapping the rope. The bucket hung from a four-wheel pulley system, giving it a mechanical advantage of four. Which meant that the crew only had to use one-quarter of the force to lift the bucket than they would have needed without the pulleys.

Nikki smiled. The pulleys reminded her of Gwen and how critical Gwen had been of the two-wheeled pulleys used by Darius and his stonemasons back in Linnea's village. Gwen had been right, of course. Four-wheeled pulleys would have made the job of fixing that broken chimney a lot easier.

She wondered where Gwen was now. Hopefully safe in the mansion of the Prince of Physics along with Athena and Fuzz. Nikki frowned up at the rocky headland above them. She couldn't see the Prince's mansion from here, but she knew it was close to the Southern Castle. The torches on the Castle's battlements were burning brightly and she could see the dark shadows of guards patrolling along the top of the massive walls. The last time she'd been in Kingston the Prince's mansion had been surrounded by the Knights of the Iron Fist. She wondered what kind of reception they were going to get this time.

Chapter Six

Refuge

"**O**UT OF MY way you treasonous tin-pot tramps!" Griff glared up at the leader of the Knights of the Iron Fist, one hand on the sword hanging from her belt. "The Prince is my kin and I have every right to visit him!"

Nikki wished Griff would stop yelling. They were outnumbered ten to one. Not to mention that the Knights were on horseback and clad in steel armor. She also wished Griff had used the secret tunnel that Curio had told her about in order to get to the Prince's mansion. Instead Griff had left her crew down on the docks and had marched straight up to the Prince's front gate. Kira, Krill, Curio and Nikki were with her. Nikki had snatched up a cloak she'd found on the ship and she had its hood pulled low over her face. Kira was standing behind Griff looking wary, but Krill and Curio were both clenching their fists and muttering under their breath. Nikki had a firm grasp on the collar of Curio's jacket. She couldn't stop Krill from doing something stupid, but she wasn't going to let Curio start a fight with fifty armed knights.

The leader of the group of knights clanked down from his horse and stepped nose to nose with Griff. "No one goes in or out of this gate," he said. "Orders of the King. Now get back to your lodgings and stay there. You lot are breaking curfew and if you disobey my orders again I'll break your heads."

Griff drew her sword and Krill stepped up next to her. Kira dragged Nikki and Curio off to one side. The knights closed in on them and it looked like a fight was inevitable, when a voice suddenly came from inside the gate.

"I say, gentlemen, please remove yourselves and your steeds. You are blocking our front gate. Our visitors are unable to enter."

Nikki squinted at the dark grounds inside the gate. It was Morton, the Prince's Head Butler. He was carrying a torch and wearing the same green satin tailcoat that he'd worn the last time she'd been in the Prince's mansion.

"We are here at the orders of the King," snarled the leader of the knights, turning to face the butler.

"Well, now, I don't think that is precisely correct," replied Morton. "I have information direct from Castle Cogent which explicitly states that the Prince and any visitors he chooses to receive shall have unimpeded access to the grounds of this estate. In fact, I have a signed document from the King stating this." He pulled a roll of parchment out of his breast pocket and pushed it through the scrolled ironwork of the front gate.

The knight grabbed it and dropped it on the ground without opening it. "My orders come from up at the Southern Castle, not from Castle Cogent. This is Kingston business, not the business of some weak-kneed little courtier sniffing roses in the gardens of Castle Cogent."

"Are you refusing to follow a direct order from the King?" said a deep voice from inside the gate. The Prince of Physics, dressed in a wine-red velvet tunic and black cloak was standing next to Morton.

The knight stared silently at the Prince for a long moment, but finally moved aside. He gestured impatiently at the group of knights. "Move your horses away from the gate," he growled.

The knights rode twenty paces down the road and then turned

back to face the gate. Their leader stood where he was, watching closely as Morton the butler unlocked the gate and Griff strode through followed by Krill. Kira, Nikki and Curio darted through after them, Nikki pulling her hood down even lower.

The Prince was silent as he and Morton led the way up the long gravel drive. They passed through the estate's rose gardens, the sweet smell of the flowers wafting up into the night air. Marble fountains splashed in the moonlight. The sea could be heard crashing against the rocky headland below. The Prince's estate was a lovely place to relax and enjoy yourself in, if you could forget about the armed knights surrounding its walls.

They passed through the grand arched entranceway of the main house where tiny figures of the Prince's ancestors were carved into the granite walls. The Prince led them down a long hallway with polished parquet floors and tapestry-covered walls. Huge bouquets of blue hydrangeas spilled out of white marble vases.

"Let's talk in the library," he said, ushering them into a room covered floor-to-ceiling with bookcases containing leather-bound books and scrolls of parchment. Heavy velvet draperies covered the windows.

"Morton, some food and drink for our guests," said the Prince.

Morton nodded and left, shutting the door behind him.

"Please, be seated," said the Prince, indicating a group of arm-chairs arranged in front of the fireplace.

Krill busied himself with starting a fire while Curio darted off to examine a globe on a bronze pedestal in a far corner of the room. Griff and Kira took chairs next to the Prince while Nikki removed her cloak and stood behind Kira's chair. A quick glance around the room showed her that no one else was there. She fought back a twinge of disappointment. She'd been hoping to see Athena and Fuzz there, eager to be reunited.

The Prince seemed to sense what she was feeling. The acid scar on his face crinkled as he gave her a small smile. "I'm afraid your friends are not here," he said. "The two imps. They were here briefly. I told them when they arrived two days ago that they were welcome to stay as long as they wanted, but Morton informed me this morning that they had scaled the wall of the back garden and disappeared. One of my cooks spotted them when she was picking some apples for breakfast just before daybreak."

Griff frowned. "Do you think they were seen by the knights?"

The Prince shook his head. "I don't believe so. I have an inform-ant among the ranks of the Knights of the Iron Fist. He would have sent word to me at once if they'd been captured. The imps picked a good spot to go over the wall. It's also the spot they used when they arrived. The walls of my estate curve around a steep rocky hillside just at that point, a piece of the same headland the Southern Castle sits on. It is the only part of my walls that the Knights can't ride their horses next to. They have mounted patrols constantly circling my estate, but at that spot they are forced to turn around. The hillside is too steep for horses."

Nikki cleared her throat nervously. "So it was just Fuzz and Athe-na who were here? Gwen wasn't . . ." She stopped, suddenly remembering that Gwen and the Prince had never met. "There wasn't a young woman with them? Long blonde hair, very pale skin, a little taller than me and a few years older."

The Prince shook his head. "No, no one was with them."

Nikki was worried, but tried to hide it. Hopefully Gwen was somewhere safe with Linnea and Darius. She wondered why the group had split up. They would have been safer staying together. After all, Gwen was just as hunted as she was. Rufius had already held Gwen captive in the Southern Castle in order to force her to make gunpowder for him. And Avaricious was searching the Realm for Gwen for the same reason. When she'd been kidnapped from the blackberry patch by Dolor and brought to Avaricious's workshop it had really been Gwen they'd wanted.

"What did the imps want?" asked Kira.

"They wanted my help in rescuing a band of imps being held in the dungeons of the Southern Castle," said the Prince. "I was sympathetic, of course. Undoubtedly the imps did nothing wrong. I don't know the reason for their imprisonment but I am certain that Rufius had a hand in it. He has ordered attacks on imp communities for no reason at all. I don't know whether he personally hates all imps, or whether he is just using them as a convenient political target. I suspect the latter."

The door opened suddenly. Griff, Kira, and Nikki jumped, but it was just Morton bearing a tray of cheese and fruit, a bottle of wine, and a silver pitcher. He set these down on a small table in front of the Prince and opened the wine with a corkscrew. The Prince poured a glass of wine for Griff and himself and glasses of apple juice out of the pitcher for the rest.

"The fire is quite hot enough, young man," the Prince said to Krill. "Leave off fussing with it and come join us."

Krill grinned and scooped up a small round of cheddar off the tray. He plopped down into a chair next to Kira, pulled out a pocket knife and began carving the wax rind off the cheese. "That wine sure smells good," he said. "Right from your own vineyards, I'm sure. I think I'll just have me a glass."

The Prince looked at him uncertainly.

Nikki grinned. She knew from her last visit to Kingston that Krill had quite a gambling habit. He'd undoubtedly been in dice games in every tavern in Kingston and had drunk more wine and ale than was good for him. Kira had told her the first time they met that she and Krill were twins. And since Kira was still a teenager that meant Krill was too, even though he didn't look it with his broad shoulders and imposing height.

"He'll have apple juice," said Griff, pouring a glass from the pitcher and handing it to him.

Krill took the glass as if it was poison. "C'mon Captain. I've drunk more bottles of wine and ale than I kin count. Won a drinking contest down at the Pig and Poke only last week. It came down to me and One-legged Tom, and at the end I was still standing and old Tom was passed out behind the bar."

"Yes," said Griff, "and as I recall you staggered out of the Pig and Poke and walked straight off a pier. If that old woman who was mending codfish nets hadn't jumped in after you you'd have drowned."

Nikki giggled, earning a half-embarrassed, half-irritated glance from Krill.

Curio rushed up suddenly, grabbed a handful of grapes from the tray and threw himself down on the carpet in front of the fire. "Mmm, lovely," he said with his mouth full.

The Prince handed him a glass of apple juice. "Thank you Morton. You may retire for the night. Just have a quick glance out the front gate first to see what our watchers are up to."

Morton nodded. "Certainly sir. I shall take Cook with me. She has saved a large basin of dishwater which is of a most satisfying greasiness. I believe it will add a nice shine to the armor of the knights once Cook dumps it on their heads. She has become quite adept at climbing the apple-picking ladder whilst holding the basin with one hand. I believe it was one of the gardeners who mentioned to her that the ladder was the perfect height for disposing of refuse over the wall."

The Prince looked like he couldn't decide whether to laugh or frown. "Just keep her away from the gate, Morton. I don't want one of the knights to exceed his orders and shoot an arrow at her."

Morton nodded solemnly and left.

The Prince sighed. "My staff is growing increasingly restless at the estate being under siege. Most of them live here in the servants' quarters, but a few walk in every day from town. There have been unpleasant rumors of the knights harassing the young women on my staff as they walk up the road to my gate. It is an intolerable situation. But unfortunately I find myself at an impasse. I have just enough power, followers and influence in Kingston to keep my estate safe from invasion, but not enough to order the knights to leave."

Griff swirled the wine in the bottom of her glass, gazing at it as if it were a crystal ball. "I wish I knew how to help. Me and my crew haven't paid as much attention to events in Kingston as we should have. We're out on the sea most of the time, so the problems in the city don't affect us much. It does surprise me though, that the people of Kingston have turned control of their city over to Rufius without a fight."

"They didn't fight for the simple reason that Rufius has been paying them," said the Prince. "Bribes right and left. Bribes to the City Council, bribes to the merchants and shopkeepers, bribes to the ship captains. And very large bribes to the Knights of the Iron Fist. I'm not certain where Rufius is getting all this money. As I understand it, he is the son of a cheese monger from Popularnum and not a wealthy man. Possibly he's stealing funds from the royal treasury. He has wormed his way into the King's favor and has gained access to all parts of the Southern Castle, including the treasury. I found Rufius oily and untrustworthy when we first met, but it appears he has very strong powers of charm and manipulation, especially among soft-hearted people like the King."

Nikki thought that the King was more soft-headed than soft-hearted, but she kept quiet. Most of his subjects, including the Prince, seemed fond of him. She wasn't sure if that was due to his personal qualities or if it was just tradition to respect the royal family. Personally she didn't think much of traditions that required you to respect nincompoops, but she wasn't going to say so. This wasn't her world.

"The King was here in the city the last time we were in port," said Griff. "Can't we just appeal to him directly? If he were to come down here in person and order the Knights to leave they would have no choice but to obey. If they refused they'd be committing treason. Me and my crew can go up to the castle and try to gain an audience with him. I've never met him but I hear he is an honorable man and open to meeting with citizens of the Realm."

The Prince shook his head. "The King has gone back to Castle Cogent. He prefers its lovely white marble walls and splashing fountains to the grim battlements of the Southern Castle. He has left Rufius in charge of the city as head of the City Council. For a while Rufius was cautious. He was patient and didn't try to impose himself on the citizens. Most of the residents of Kingston didn't even know he had been put in charge. But lately he has made himself unpopular. He has raised taxes and imposed harsh new laws. There is a curfew now. All residents must be in their homes before midnight. The fee for tying up a ship at the docks has tripled, and I suspect these fat fees are going straight into Rufius's hands. I let many captains such as yourself use my private dock, but I doubt I'll be able to continue that for much longer. The Knights of the Iron Fist have threatened to barricade my dock, which would be very easy to do. Of course, Rufius is always careful to say he does all this in the King's name, but the people are becoming restless and even rebellious. I fear there may be violence in the city before long. I have done what I could to keep the peace, but with the King gone and the Knights of the Iron Fist surrounding my estate my influence is lessening by the day."

Griff frowned into her wineglass but didn't speak.

"Well," said the Prince, rising from his chair. "We are not going to solve all of Kingston's problems tonight. I will ask Morton to prepare bedrooms for all of you. Please stay as long as you want. It is nice to have the company. As you can imagine, I get few visitors these days."

NIKKI GROANED AND punched her pillow. She'd been trying to get to sleep for hours with no luck. The night before had been just as sleepless. Her worries about Fuzz, Athena, and Gwen were gnawing at her. As an outsider she didn't understand all the things going on in the Realm, but she knew the situation was getting worse, not just in Kingston but all over. All imps in the Realm had become targets, and Gwen was being hunted by powerful people who wanted her to make weapons for them.

At breakfast that morning she'd tried to persuade the Prince to send someone up to the Southern Castle to find out if Fuzz and Athena were there, either as guests or as prisoners. But the Prince had refused. He'd said that any emissary he sent up to the castle would be in danger of arrest. Griff and Kira had said the same thing. Krill had offered to go, but Griff had swatted him on the head with a map of Kingston she'd been studying and ordered him to go help the Prince's gardeners dig up potatoes for dinner.

Griff and the Prince were trying to come up with a plan to stop Rufius from completely taking over Kingston. They'd been shut in the library all day studying maps of the city and the Southern Castle. Nikki knew that freeing the city from Rufius was important, but right now she was more concerned with the safety of her friends. She couldn't just lie in bed while they were in danger. She threw off the covers and climbed out of bed. She snatched her Westlake Debate Team T-Shirt off the bedpost and sniffed it. It didn't smell too bad. One of the Prince's staff had washed it for her. She put it on under the black suede tunic Kira had loaned her and pulled on her borrowed black trousers and her Nikes. She threw on her cloak and carefully opened the door of the bedroom, wincing at the squeak from its hinges. Far off, down the long hallway which led to the servant's quarters, she could hear people moving about and talking quietly. One of the voices sounded like Morton the butler. The staff was still up. It would be hard to get all the way to the front door without being seen.

She quietly shut her door and hurried across the room to the balcony. She opened its glass-paned door and stepped out into the night. Frost covered the tiles of the small terrace and Nikki shivered as she cautiously leaned over the balcony railing. Her room was only on the second floor and the drop to the gardens below didn't look that far. She darted back inside and grabbed the linen sheet off her bed. After she tied it to the balcony railing she gave it a sharp tug. It seemed secure. She climbed over the railing, grabbed the sheet with both hands, and stepped out into thin air. The sheet twisted around in a spiral as soon as she hung her weight on it. The spinning bashed her knees hard against a marble column of the balcony below hers. Nikki bit her lip to keep from crying out and inched down the spiraling sheet. The sheet didn't quite reach the ground and she had to drop the last few feet, tumbling head over heels into a bed of frost-rimmed begonias. She spit out a begonia leaf and dusted herself off. There was no outcry from the mansion. No one seemed to have noticed her awkward exit.

She kept a sharp eye out for the Prince's guards as she ran across the front lawn of the estate and into the rose garden. The splashing from the garden's many fountains masked the crunching of her feet on the gravel paths. She spotted a few dark figures patrolling along the walls of the estate, but their attention was focused outward, alert to any incursions from the Knights of the Iron Fist. They weren't paying much attention to the interior of the estate and Nikki had no problem reaching the back gardens. Vegetables for the kitchen were grown here and Nikki hunkered down behind a row of string beans while she surveyed the back wall of the estate.

The steep hillside the Prince had mentioned loomed up like the prow of a ship about to crash through the back wall. The hill was definitely too steep for horses, but it looked climbable by a person. If Fuzz and Athena could do it then so could she. She'd hoped to find the cook's apple-picking ladder leaning conveniently against the wall, but she didn't see it anywhere.

She squinted at the wall. It was about twenty feet in height, built out of large blocks of rough stone. The ladder would have been nice, but she was pretty sure she could manage without it. She took one last glance around. No one was in sight. She dashed up to the wall and stuck her fingers into a crack in the wall above her head. By digging her toes and fingers into the wall she managed to get halfway up without much trouble. A smooth spot in the middle with no hand or foot holds gave her several minutes of difficult scrambling, but finally she reached the top and pulled herself up and over. Climbing down the other side was easier. The drop was short as the hillside touched the wall at that point. At the bottom she flattened herself against the wall, listening for the clip-clop of horses' hooves.

The night was still. An owl hooted far off in the distance and a cat yowled down in the city, but otherwise everything was quiet. The waves crashing down below the headland were a soothing background noise. Nikki breathed a sigh of relief and began her assault on the rocky hillside.

Fortunately the moon was full, for it was difficult going and she needed the light. The hillside consisted of hard, jagged stones which had shifted and cracked over the eons into dozens of narrow gullies only a few feet wide. Jumping across the gaps was terrifying. She couldn't see how deep they were, and more than once she nearly lost her balance and fell in.

After an hour's hard climbing she glanced up and saw that the outer battlements of the Southern Castle were much closer than before. She could hear the clink of the guards' armor as they patrolled along the top of the wall. Huge fiery torches were set on the wall, illuminating the strip of land in front of the castle like a moat made of light. It would be almost impossible to get across that band of light without being seen.

Nikki sat down on top of a rock and stared at the looming castle, the guards, and the torches. Fuzz and Athena couldn't possibly have gotten into the castle from this side. Even if they'd somehow gone unseen the walls were over a hundred feet high and made of smooth stone with no hand or foot holds. She also doubted that they'd entered by the front gate. It was heavily guarded, and now that the King had left they no longer had his protection.

The section of wall which Gwen had blown up with gunpowder suddenly leapt to her mind. The destroyed section might not have been re-built yet, and the rubble from the fallen piece of wall would give her cover. She squinted up at the dark towers of the castle. She wasn't sure where the destroyed section was. It was a huge fortress, probably half a mile long, and she wasn't very familiar with its layout.

She had just decided to try going around the castle in the opposite direction from the front gate when she heard the faintest whisper of voices. She froze, listening. The whispers were coming from directly below her, at the bottom of a pitch black gully. She ducked down, lying flat on the rock and inching forward until she could see over the edge. She couldn't see anyone, but the whispers continued to float up to her. She inched a bit farther forward.

"Miss, you are going to fall in if you are not careful."

Nikki gasped, her heart pounding through her chest. She felt a small hand pat her on the shoulder.

"It is all right, Miss. It is just me."

Nikki sat up. Athena was standing on the rock next to her.

"What . . . how . . . oh my gosh you scared me" gasped Nikki.

"Miss, we must leave this rock at once. It is not safe. The guards on the battlements use spyglasses which allow them to see long distances. They might spot us even in the dark. Come. We will join the others down below."

Chapter Seven

Rescue of the Prisoners

"**I** STILL CAN'T believe you managed to get to Kingston all by yourself," said Fuzz, his mouth full of the biscuit he was munching on.

"Well, I did," said Nikki. "It was kind of scary, but I managed it."

She was sitting in the bottom of the gully on a cold and uncomfortable rock. Cation was purring away in her lap, kneading Nikki's leg with her sharp little claws. Fuzz, Athena, and Linnea were huddled on nearby rocks with their cloaks wrapped around them.

"That little fuzz ball is certainly glad to see you," said Linnea. "She wasn't happy to have me carting her around in my herb bag. She kept sneezing. Probably because of the dried ragwort, or maybe the chamomile blossoms. She gave me more than one scratch, let me tell you."

"Sorry about that," said Nikki. "She doesn't always have the best manners." She scratched Cation under the chin and the kitten stretched out her legs and purred even louder. She'd grown since the last time Nikki had seen her. Instead of being a round, furry toddler she now had the long legs of a teenager.

A squeaking sound echoed off the rock walls of the gully and a tiny white mouse popped its head out of Linnea's sleeve and scrambled up her arm to perch on her head. The mouse aimed a fierce squeak in

Cation's direction and Cation responded with a low growl.

Nikki grabbed the kitten with both hands to prevent Rosie from becoming Cation's after dinner treat.

Linnea laughed. "It's okay. These two have been trading insults for days but nothing has ever happened. You kitten has been feeding off of field mice this whole trip. She's quite the mouser. But she seems to consider Rosie a sparring partner rather than a meal."

Cation let out a loud yowl that signaled her superiority over all mice, then she settled back into kneading Nikki's leg like a loaf of bread.

"Miss, your kitten is making quite a bit of noise," said Athena. "Can you make her be quiet?"

"Oh relax," said Fuzz. "No one can hear us way down here."

"Miss Nikki heard us," Athena pointed out.

"She was right above us," said Fuzz. "There's no one else on this entire headland. Too hard to climb, too easy to fall into one of these blasted gullies."

"You might be right," said Nikki, "but if the Prince knows the exact spot where you went over his wall then the Knights of the Iron Fist might know too." She'd told them as much as she could remember about the conversation between Griff and the Prince of Physics.

Fuzz snorted. "Those tin-pot knights are way too lazy to climb this headland. They prefer parading around the city on their horses, bullying the locals. Nope, we have this place to ourselves, as long as Gwen and Darius don't lead the palace guards back here."

"I'm sure they are staying out of sight," said Athena. "The guards will not spot them."

"Where are they anyway?" asked Nikki.

"They're on a scouting trip," said Fuzz. "We've been taking turns going all around the castle, trying to find a way in so we can rescue the imps imprisoned in the dungeons. We think they're a band that escaped from imp headquarters in the Trackless Forest, when the

Knights of the Iron Fist attacked it and drove us out of the tunnels with smoke. Our first thought for a way into the Southern Castle to rescue them was that big hole Gwen blew in the outer wall, up on the east side of the battlements. But it's been repaired already. I was mighty surprised, let me tell you. The palace guards aren't usually that efficient. It was probably Rufius's doing. He's been fortifying the castle. Strengthening the watch towers, adding more archers and more canons. The place wasn't such a fortress when the King was in residence. The King likes rose gardens, good food, and parties, but Rufius is really into military stuff. He likes power, that one. He's mostly confined himself to manipulation so far, but it looks like he's getting ready to seize power by force."

"Yes, yes," said Athena impatiently. "Rufius is a very bad man. There is no need to dwell on what everyone already knows. What *I* want to know is what happened to Miss Nikki. One moment we were all asleep in the middle of a blackberry patch, and the next moment Miss Nikki had disappeared."

Nikki pulled Cation's claws out of her leg. "It was Dolor. The tooth puller. He snatched me out of the blackberry patch and took me all the way to Deceptionville. To Avaricious's workshop. Avaricious is still under the delusion that I can make special potions, turn lead into gold, that sort of nonsense. He's also looking for Gwen, by the way. For the same reason. He's got Lurkers out searching for her."

"Yes, we know," said Linnea. "One of the farmers from my village told us. Many people in my village bring their crops into Kingston to sell in the market. We stopped there and I got all the latest news and gossip from home. It seems that several Lurkers broke into my cottage and searched it. They frightened my cook and broke my mother's best china plates. They got their comeuppance, though. My parrot Samson swooped down on them and raked one of them across the forehead with his claws and nearly bit the other one's nose off with his beak."

"Yes, that was very amusing to hear," said Athena. "But let us get back to you, Miss. You were not hurt by that nasty Dolor or that greedy Avaricious?"

Nikki shook her head. "No, I'm fine. I managed to escape from Avaricious's workshop pretty quickly, and I ended up hiding in Deceptionville's City Hall for a few days. In the laboratory of an old alchemist called Geber."

Fuzz laughed. "Good old Geber. What a pile of crotchety old bones. Calls himself the official alchemist of Deceptionville, but it's been many years since anyone paid any attention to him."

"By the way," said Linnea. "It's not just Gwen the Lurkers are after. We saw wanted posters of you in the market here in Kingston."

"Yes, the posters all over Deceptionville too," said Nikki. "I seem to have gotten lots of people in the Realm mad at me. Even Fortuna the Fortunate. By the way, Fortuna is pretty much running Deceptionville now, along with Avaricious. Deceptionville's mayor was found dead a few weeks ago, drowned in the river, and Fortuna saw her chance. She's taken over the city council and the King's rooms at City Hall. And she's also selling a potion called Lily of the Night. It's very dangerous. It has lead in it, which is very toxic. People who use her potion are going to get very ill, even die, if we don't do something."

Fuzz yanked on his hair. "Aargh. One crisis at a time. I promise we'll try to do something about Fortuna, but right now we have to concentrate on getting the imps out of the castle dungeon before Rufius does something nasty to them."

Nikki was about to add to Fuzz's frustration by telling him about the strange men from the Mystic Mountains who had a grudge against the King, when a rattle of stones sounded in the gully.

Fuzz jumped off his rock and grabbed a wooden cudgel which was leaning against the rock wall.

They all listened tensely until a quiet whisper came floating along the winding gully.

"It's just us."

Nikki breathed a sigh of relief and Fuzz put down his cudgel. It was Gwen's voice.

Gwen appeared around a bend in the gully, her pale blond hair shining faintly in the darkness. Darius the stonecutter was right behind her. "Nikki!" Gwen exclaimed.

Nikki jumped up to give her a hug and to shake hands with Darius, whose large hand felt like he cleaned it with sandpaper.

Gwen dropped the leather bag she was carrying on the ground and sat down on a rock. Fuzz handed her a biscuit.

"So," said Fuzz, "any success?"

Gwen shook her head. "No. We went all the way around the perimeter this time. There's just no way in. The only entrance is the front gate, which has a whole troop of guards in front of it. And the walls are too high to climb. At first I thought we might be able to use a crossbow to shoot a rope up and latch onto a battlement, then climb up. But the guards are doing regular patrols all along the battlements. They'd spot us immediately."

"What about that tunnel we used last time?" asked Nikki. "The one that runs from the Prince's mansion up to his old laboratory inside the castle?"

Fuzz shook his head. "Nah, the Knights of the Iron Fist know about that one. They blocked it up at the castle end with big boulders. Me and Athena tried it a few days ago when we stayed with the Prince." He let out a sigh. "That tunnel starts in the Prince's wine cellar. What a collection. Treats himself well, the Prince does. Me, I'm more of an ale man, but I don't mind a drop of the grape now and then. I don't mind telling you I did a bit of sampling while I was down in the Prince's cellar. There was a particular vintage . . ."

Athena threw a biscuit at Fuzz, which bounced off his head. "Never mind your samplings and gluggings. We are on a mission. The lives of our friends in the castle dungeons depend on us."

"There's another tunnel," said Nikki. "Curio told me about it. He was on Griff's ship when Griff and her crew rescued me out in the middle of the ocean. It's a long story. Anyway, Curio says this other tunnel starts at the Prince's dock and goes up to the castle."

"Really?" said Fuzz. "I've never heard about it. Then again, I'm not that close to the Prince. The Prince stays in Kingston most of the time, while me and old Athena here bounce all over the Realm on the King's business."

"Curio says he heard about the tunnel from Krill," said Nikki. "Griff probably told Krill about it. And Griff is a relative of the Prince's, so I guess it makes sense that he would tell her."

"Hmm," said Fuzz. "Well, I don't know how much we should depend on something Curio says. He means well, but he has the brains of a bumblebee. Still, I guess it's worth checking out. It's not like we have any other options."

Fuzz hopped down from his rock and picked up his cudgel. The others gathered up their bags and rucksacks. Nikki tucked Cation on her shoulder. The kitten fastened her claws onto Nikki's cloak and purred loudly in her ear.

It took them much less time to go down the headland than it had for Nikki to climb up it. Fuzz seemed to know every path and gully. Many of the narrow little canyons were connected if you knew where to look. It seemed like a hugely complex maze to Nikki, but in short order they found themselves hiding behind a boulder staring warily out at the Prince's wooden pier. Griff's ship was still tied to the end of it, rocking gently in the moonlight, but none of the crew was in sight. An owl was hooting off in the distance, and Griff's ship creaked as it swayed and bumped against the pier, but otherwise the night was quiet.

"Curio didn't mention how to spot the entrance to this mysterious tunnel, did he?" whispered Fuzz.

"No," said Nikki. "I guess we'll just have to search for it."

"Wait," said Darius, holding up a large hand. "I hear water trickling nearby. Sounds like an underground stream. Stay here." He disappeared into the darkness.

Nikki settled herself on the ground to wait, but Darius was back in only a few minutes.

"I've found the entrance," he said. "It's carefully concealed and a very tight fit, but I believe we can squeeze through."

Darius led them back up the hill a short ways and then into the narrowest gully they'd entered so far. Nikki's shoulders touched the sides of the vertical rock walls, and Darius had to walk sideways. As they went deeper in Nikki could hear what Darius had noticed – a quiet rushing sound, just barely audible over the ocean waves crashing against the shoreline behind them. The gully made a confusing series of turns and branches, then ended at a rock wall covered with thorn bushes growing out of its vertical face.

Darius put on a pair of leather gloves he had hanging from his belt and pulled back the thorn bushes. A narrow crack in the rock wall about four feet high revealed itself. A light mist floated out from the crack.

"Sounds like a waterfall," said Fuzz.

"Yes," said Darius. "Probably an underground stream or river which empties into the sea." He knelt down and opened the bag of stonemason tools he carried. There was a brief flash of light as he struck a piece of flint on the rock wall of the gully. The sparks caught on the leaves of a thorn bush. Darius pulled three candles from his bag and quickly lit them. He handed one to Fuzz and one to Nikki, then smothered the fire with a handful of dirt. "Shall we?" he said, holding his candle aloft and awkwardly squeezing into the tunnel entrance.

Nikki followed. Cation jumped down from her shoulder and darted ahead into the darkness. Their candles threw strange shapes on the jagged walls. The sandy floor of the tunnel was damp and there was a strong smell of decayed seaweed. At one point the walls closed in so tightly that Nikki had to turn sideways. Up ahead she could hear Darius grunting as he tried to shove himself through the narrow gap. She paused, wondering if the stonemason was going to get stuck, but after a bit of grunting and cursing he managed to squeeze through and she saw his candle move forward again.

The tunnel ended in a tiny underground beach. They all collected on the sand and squinted into the darkness. They were on the edge of a small black pool. The rushing sound they'd heard was a waterfall, not more than knee-height, which flowed out of the pool and toward the ocean. Cation was high-stepping along the sand, delicately shaking her wet feet and looking sulky.

Nikki breathed a sigh of relief as she studied the current flowing across the pool. It was very slow. The pool was fed by a sluggish stream, not the terrifying, rushing river she'd encountered inside the Mystic Mountains. Her candle picked out a strange shape at the far end of the little beach and she went over to investigate.

Gwen joined her. "It looks like a pump," she said.

Nikki nodded. "There's a pipe leading from it into the water. It looks like it's used to drain the tunnel." She leaned over the pool and held her candle above her head. "Look, there's also an Archimedes screw and what I think is an inverted siphon."

"A what?" asked Gwen. "I've seen these screws before. They're pretty common in low-lying areas. Farmers use them to drain flood water off their fields. But I've never heard of an inverted siphon."

"They're used to pull water uphill," said Nikki. She pointed at a bronze pipe shaped like an upside-down letter 'U'. "See how the tunnel slopes down right here, at the end of the pool? There's a path along the side of the pool, but it's covered by water at the bottom of the slope. It looks like someone set up this inverted siphon to pull water up from the tunnel into this pool so it can drain out into the ocean."

"It's probably an invention of the Prince of Physics," said Gwen, lifting the wooden lid off the top of the pump and peering inside. "It's too bad he isn't with us. I don't think this pump is working." She tried pushing on the handle sticking out of the top of the pump, but nothing happened.

Nikki held her candle over the pump and looked inside. "We should be able to get it working again. It's just a standard piston pump. It uses suction to pump water. Griff has one just like it in the hold of her ship." She held her candle closer to the cylinder inside the pump's outer housing. "I see the problem. The connecting rod has come loose from the piston. It looks like they're both made of bronze. We just need something which can melt bronze. Then we could weld the two pieces back together again."

"I could do it easily if I was back in my workshop in D-ville," said Gwen. "But here? We don't have a furnace."

Athena came up and peered inside the pump. "Miss, let us check the water level in the tunnel first. We may not need this apparatus if the water is shallow enough to wade through."

"I'll check," said Darius. "If I can get through then I can help the rest across the deep parts."

They watched nervously as Darius dropped his stonemason's bag on the sand and started down the narrow path along the edge of the pool. His candle was soon just a pinpoint of light as the path sloped down into the hillside. They heard a small splash as he waded into the water.

"I don't know about anyone else," said Linnea, her voice shaking a little, "but I can't swim."

"I can dogpaddle," said Gwen.

"I'm a strong swimmer," said Nikki, hoping she didn't sound conceited.

"I learned to swim in the lake near our house when I was a child," said Athena. "But Fuzz cannot swim. I had to pull him out of the Deceptionville River once. By his hair. He fell in after one of his many visits to the Wolf's Hide tavern. He came to the surface with so many cursings and spittings that he scared away some men who were fishing nearby. They thought I had caught a river demon."

Fuzz shrugged. "Okay, so maybe I can't exactly swim. I have lots of other talents."

"Darius could give you a ride on his shoulders," suggested Nikki.

Fuzz didn't look too happy about this idea, but his response was interrupted by the sight of a soaking-wet Darius climbing back up the slope toward them. He plopped down on the sand.

"Had to swim underwater," he said, trying to catch his breath. "The top of the tunnel meets the water not far ahead. The whole tunnel is flooded. I swam as far as I could, but had to turn around before I ran out of air. Looks like we either have to get that pump working or give up on this as a way into the castle."

"Oh dear," said Athena. "There are not any other ways in. We have looked and looked."

"Do you mind if I look inside your bag?" Nikki asked Darius.

"Sure," he said. "Help yourself."

Nikki rummaged in the heavy leather stonemason bag, pulling out the flint Darius had used to light the candles. She set that aside and nodded in satisfaction when she discovered a small greased bag filled with chunks of charcoal. "A bellows!" she exclaimed when she pulled out a fan-shaped, accordion-like object about a foot in length.

"You're going to build a furnace," said Gwen.

"Yes," said Nikki. She handed Fuzz a bricklayer's spade which she pulled out of the bag. "Fuzz, would you dig a hole in a dry spot? About five inches across and a foot deep."

Fuzz nodded and went searching for a dry spot in the sand.

"What are you going to use for solder?" asked Gwen.

"That extra bit of pipe sticking out of the side of the pump. I'm not sure what it's for, maybe an overflow valve, but I don't think it's critical." She pulled a hammer out of the bag. "Darius, do you think you can knock that piece off?"

Darius took the hammer and knocked the piece off as if it had been made of butter instead of bronze.

Nikki took the flint, charcoal, and bellows over to the hole Fuzz had dug and felt inside it. "It's still a bit damp. We need something to line it with."

Linnea pulled a big handful of dried mustard stalks out of her herb bag and spread them in the bottom of the hole.

Nikki dumped the charcoal on top and added a few mustard stalks for kindling. She hit the flint hard against the rock wall of the tunnel as she'd seen Darius do. Sparks flew at once and she caught one on a stalk of dried mustard. She held the flaming stalk against the pile of charcoal until the coals started to smoke. "We need something to cover the hole with. To keep the heat in."

Athena rummaged in her rucksack and handed Nikki a tiny grey woolen dress identical to the one she had on.

Nikki tucked the dress tightly over the hole and weighted it down with rocks, leaving a small opening on one side. The she pushed the nozzle of the bellows into the hole and pumped the bellows up and down. She could feel the heat from the charcoal rise instantly.

"You'll need something to put the bronze in," said Gwen, pulling a tin drinking cup out of her own rucksack.

Nikki put the piece of bronze pipe into the cup and lifted the hole's cover just enough to tuck the cup on top of the now bright red coals.

It didn't take long. After a few minutes Nikki put on one of Darius's leather gloves and lifted the cover off the hole. When she picked up the tin cup the melted bronze sloshed around inside it like thick hot chocolate. She set it down in the sand to cool slightly.

Gwen picked up the little hand-bellows. "It's always amazed me how a little extra air can make a fire so much hotter. I've asked a few of the alchemists in D-ville, but no one seems to know why."

"There's an element in air called oxygen which is very reactive," said Nikki. "It reacts with the fuel source, in this case charcoal, to cause an exothermic chain reaction called combustion. Exothermic just means it gives off heat." She paused and looked around guiltily. She was bringing twenty-first century knowledge to the Realm again. Luckily everyone else except Gwen had wandered off, putting some distance between themselves and the smell of Athena's burning wool dress.

Gwen peered into the nozzle of the bellows. "So this oxygen is contained in the bellows?"

"No," said Nikki. "Oxygen is part of the air. The bellows just uses pressure to increase the supply of air available to the fire."

"Hmm," said Gwen. "When I heat something in my workshop in D-ville I've noticed that the fire sometimes gives off water vapor. Does that have something to do with this oxygen substance?"

Nikki nodded. "Yes. Oxygen in the air combines with another substance called hydrogen, which is in the charcoal, to create water vapor. Water is made up of one bit of oxygen for every two bits of hydrogen. We call these atoms or elements in my world." She peered inside the cooling cup of liquid bronze. "We'd better get started on the welding before this cools too much."

Nikki applied the solder while Darius and Gwen held the piston and connecting rod steady. The weld wasn't very professional looking. It looked like a big clump of cookie dough that had baked into a weird shape. But Nikki thought that the weld would hold. She poured a bit of water from Gwen's tin cup on it to cool it down and gave an experimental push on the handle of the pump.

Nothing happened.

"You need more force," said Darius. He pushed down on the handle with both hands and a strange sucking noise echoed around the cave. After a few more pushes they could all see that the water level in the pool was rising and the noise of the little waterfall was louder.

"It's working," called Fuzz, standing on the edge of the pool and peering into the tunnel. "The water's dropping."

They could hear water gurgling up the inverted siphon and see it spiraling up the helix of the Archimedes screw. The suction pump was obviously connected to them somehow, but the connection mechanism was hidden under the pool of water.

It took nearly an hour, with Linnea, Nikki, and Gwen taking turns at the pump to give Darius an occasional break.

"Well," gasped Darius, rubbing his lower back. "It looks like we've done it. Handy contraption, that pump, but I'd like to have a few words with this Prince of yours if I ever meet him. He needs to make his inventions a bit easier on the back. I'm not made of iron."

Gwen patted him on the arm and handed him his bag. "Maybe not, but you do come in handy."

Darius grinned down at her. "Well, we'd better be going. I'm not too proud to admit that I'm not looking forward to this rescue. Seems harebrained and risky to me. I just want to get it over with and go back to my village."

Fuzz nodded and led the way down into the tunnel. Athena, Gwen and Linnea followed.

"What's the matter young Miss?" Darius asked Nikki as she hesitated.

"It's just that I've lost my . . ."

Cation suddenly launched herself from a ledge on the cave wall and pounced on Nikki, teetering precariously on her shoulder. Nikki winced as the sharp little claws dug through her cloak. "Never mind," she said and started down into the tunnel.

"SSSHHH", WHISPERED FUZZ. "I can hear voices." He raised the candle he was carrying and peered into the dark tunnel ahead of them.

Everyone stopped in their tracks. They were deep under the Southern Castle and they were all wet from the knees down. They'd had to wade through water in parts of the tunnel, but fortunately the pump had done its job and the water had been shallow. No one had been forced to swim. Except Cation. She'd misjudged a leap from Nikki's shoulder to the tunnel floor and had landed right in a deep puddle. She'd spent the rest of the trip through the tunnel dripping cold water onto Nikki's neck and mewling pitifully.

"Shut that blasted cat up," hissed Fuzz as Cation let out a particularly loud complaint.

Nikki hastily shoved Cation into Athena's rucksack and closed the drawstring top. The rucksack growled quietly for a minute and then was still.

"The voices seem to be right over our heads," said Darius, holding his candle up and peering at the ceiling. The top of the tunnel was low enough for him to touch it.

Fuzz handed his candle to Athena and pulled a folded piece of parchment out of his trouser pocket. He opened it and motioned everyone to gather around.

Athena held the candle over it and traced a line on the parchment with her finger. "I believe we have arrived at the correct spot," she said. "We are directly under the deepest part of the dungeon. We borrowed this map from the library in the Prince's mansion. We weren't aware of this tunnel at that time, but we thought the map might come in handy if we managed to somehow scale the castle walls."

They all looked from the map up to the ceiling. The voices were a bit louder now.

Fuzz cocked his head on one side, listening carefully. "Those aren't palace guards. Those are imp voices. They're higher pitched than big-people voices, and I think I hear a couple of imp women."

Darius looked thoughtfully up at the tunnel ceiling. The tunnel's rough-hewn rock had changed to carved blocks of granite about two feet square. The stonemason pulled a spade out of his bag and chipped carefully at the crumbling mortar around one block. Bits of the mortar rained down on his head and the voices above them grew louder. "Well," he said, "I'm not sure how wise this is, but we may be able to go right up through the dungeon floor. This mortar looks like it hasn't been patched in centuries." He looked questioningly at Fuzz and Athena and they both nodded.

Darius motioned everyone to stand back and then started hacking vigorously at the mortar. In a surprisingly short time there was a pile of crumbled mortar at his feet and the block above his head was tilting ominously. Darius planted his feet, took a deep breath, and shoved hard on one edge of the block with both hands. The heavy stone tipped and swayed and then suddenly came crashing down. Darius jumped out of the way just in time. The dirt floor of the tunnel absorbed some of the sound, but the vibrations shook the tunnel walls.

Everyone held their breath, looking warily up at the black hole where the stone had been.

Suddenly something moved in the hole.

Fuzz held his candle up.

"Get that light outta my face, you nincompoop. Been locked in the dark for weeks. Can't see a blasted thing with that bonfire blinding me."

A head poked out of the hole. It had a long nose and straggly grey hair tucked in a bun on its neck.

"Aunt Gertie?" asked Athena uncertainly. "Is that you?"

The head twisted to look at her. "Athena? Well, well. It's about time girl. We've been stuck in here ever since those tin pots on horseback raided imp headquarters. Took you long enough."

The imp twisted to look at Darius. "Hey, you. Mister Giant. Catch me."

Darius just had time to jump forward and hold out his arms before the imp dropped from the hole. The cane she was holding whacked him in the face as he caught her. He quickly set her on the ground and stepped back.

Nikki, who was standing nearby, realized why. The elderly imp smelled. Badly. Nikki wasn't sure if the smell was due to two weeks in a dungeon or just the imp's natural smell, but whatever the cause it was pungent, with a whiff of onions.

The imp peered around at all of them and then suddenly hobbled briskly toward Fuzz and clobbered him over the head with her cane.

"Owwww!" yelled Fuzz, retreating to a safe distance and muttering some well-chosen swear words. "Every single time. You'd think I could manage to dodge that blasted cane by now. I've had enough practice."

"That weren't nothing," said the imp. "I'll give you more than that, you beer-guzzling good-for-nothing." She started for Fuzz again.

Athena quickly jumped in front of her. "Aunt Gertie now is not the time. You and Fuzz must save your feuds and fightings until we are safely away from here. Now, how many others are in the dungeon?"

"Eleven," said the imp. "And here comes the first one." She pointed at the hole with her cane.

A young male imp dropped nimbly out of the hole and did a somersault as he hit the dirt floor. The rest of the imps dropped with less grace, but soon all twelve of them were standing in the tunnel. Aunt Gertie was the only elderly imp, but there were two other women. All the prisoners looked dirty and hungry, but they stood calmly watching Athena and Fuzz for orders.

"Right," said Fuzz, edging around Aunt Gertie. "Well, no time for introductions. This is a rescue. Everyone follow me." He started back down the tunnel the way they'd come.

"Mister Darius, sir," said Athena. "Would you be so kind as to give my aunt a ride? She has much trouble walking."

Darius didn't look too happy about this request, but he grudgingly bent down so that the old imp could climb onto his back.

"Wait a second," said Linnea, digging around in her herb bag. "I have something which may help." She pulled out a small clay pot, dipped a finger in it and rubbed some kind of ointment under Darius's nose. "Peppermint," she said.

"Thanks," Darius said gratefully.

It didn't take them long to reach the small pool of water where they'd started. Their candles threw strange shadows across the water as they passed the pump and the inverted siphon. They squeezed out of the narrow crack which was the entrance to the tunnel and extinguished their candles in the sand of the gully floor. Everyone waited nervously as Fuzz and Athena held a whispered argument. Athena seemed to win.

"We will go by sea," she whispered, motioning them onward.

The rescued imps looked a bit confused by this announcement, but Nikki had a sinking feeling that she knew what Athena was up to. And sure enough, when they had found their way out of the maze of gullies and were again hiding behind the big boulder near the Prince's dock she saw Athena point at Griff's ship. It was still floating peacefully on the water, tied to the long pier where Griff's crew had unloaded their haul of codfish.

"I don't see anyone," whispered Fuzz. "And I don't hear any knights clanking around on their horses. Might as well make a run for it. The moon's not up yet, so we should be hard to spot from the castle."

Athena nodded and led the way onto the long wooden pier. The waves gently crashing onto the shore masked the creaking of the pier as they all scurried along it.

The ship's gangplank was pulled up but that didn't stop the imps. They all immediately swarmed up the thick ropes which tied the ship to the pier. The young ones climbed as nimbly as monkeys while the older ones followed more slowly. Soon the only ones left on the dock were Darius, Athena, Linnea, Gwen, Aunt Gertie and Nikki.

Linnea was looking doubtfully at the nearest rope. "I don't think I can manage it," she whispered. "I was never very good at climbing trees when I was younger and this looks much more difficult than climbing the old oak tree in my village."

"Not to worry," said Darius. "I'll let down a rope and you can just hang on while I pull you up." He climbed a lot more awkwardly than the imps, but he managed it eventually and heaved himself over the ship's railing. He threw down a line. Linnea caught it and hung on tightly with both hands while Darius hauled her up like a fisherman catching a trout.

"It is perhaps a bit undignified, but I will also take this way up," whispered Athena. "I am not as nimble as I was in my youth."

"Me too," said Gwen. "I could probably climb, but I think this will be faster."

"I coulda climbed twenty ropes back in the old days," said Aunt Gertie. "Still can, I bet. But I might as well make the Giant work for his supper."

Nikki nodded and left them to wait their turn. She went over to the thick swaying rope which anchored the ship to the pier and grasped it tightly with both hands. She eased herself off the pier, hanging there awkwardly until she managed to swing her legs up onto the rope. It was a difficult climb, but not impossible. It was easier than the rope climb back in her high school gym class. At least this rope didn't go straight up. The hardest part was the last bit just under the ship's railing. The rope kept slapping against the ship, banging her fingers painfully against the hull.

"Just hang there for a second," said Gwen, leaning over the railing. "Darius is almost done. He'll pull you up."

Nikki didn't have long to wait. An arm reached over the railing and grabbed her around the waist. Darius pulled her up and set her on the deck of the ship.

"Thanks," said Nikki, rubbing her bruised fingers. She joined the others, who were all gathered around the ship's wheel.

"Right," said Fuzz. "So, who knows how to sail?"

Nikki's mouth fell open. "But, this was *your* plan. Well, yours and Athena's. If you didn't know how to sail why did you get us on this ship?"

Fuzz shrugged. "I figured we could fake it. It can't be that hard." He looked around at the group. "So, any sailors?"

No one spoke.

Nikki groaned. She really, really didn't want to, but she slowly raised her hand.

"Miss!" said Athena. "You can sail this ship?"

"No," said Nikki. Her stomach sank as she looked up at the towering mast with its three huge booms and the complex web of ropes hanging from them. "No, I can't. But it looks like I'll have to try. I can sail small boats. *Very* small boats. Like that one over there." She pointed to a small rowboat leaning against some barrels in the stern.

"Wonderful!" said Fuzz, clapping her on the back. "So, you're now officially the captain. Just tell us what you want us to do."

"Mainsail," Nikki managed to say, trying not to picture the moment when she was undoubtedly going to capsize the huge ship and drown everyone on it. "We have to get the mainsail up." She peered up at the mast. "Let's try setting only one sail. The lowest one. It's furled around the first boom. Someone needs to go up there and untie the sail."

"We're on it," said Fuzz. He waved at some of the younger imps and they quickly swarmed up the rope ladders which were hanging from the mast.

After a bit of trial and error Nikki and Gwen figured out which of the dozens of ropes attached to the mast went with which sail and with Darius's help they managed to raise the lowest mainsail. It billowed out alarmingly and the ship strained against the ropes which held it to the dock.

"We'll have to cut them," said Darius, pulling out a knife from his stonemason bag and pointing to the dock lines. "Are you ready?"

Nikki gulped. "Just a second." She looked up at the sail. It was billowing out toward the ocean, which meant the wind was coming straight off the headland. And the bow of the ship was pointed out to sea. That was a lucky break. It meant she could leave the dock on a run, with the wind behind her. The ship would head straight out to sea and she wouldn't have to tack or gybe to get away from shore. She wouldn't have to worry about turning until they were way out in the ocean, where there was nothing to run into.

Nikki walked on shaky legs over to the ship's wheel and grasped it with sweaty palms. She nodded to Darius.

Darius cut the dock line in the stern and the ship tilted alarmingly. Everyone grabbed at the nearest railing and held on tight. Darius ran quickly to the bow and cut the other line. The ship surged forward, knocking Aunt Gertie off her feet.

Nikki hung onto the wheel with all her might. The ship didn't keep a completely straight line and it shuddered as the hull scraped against the pilings of the pier with an ear-piercing squeal. Nikki edged the wheel a bit to port, away from the pier. The squealing got even louder as the ship rammed the pier. Nikki swore under her breath and frantically swung the wheel to starboard. She'd forgotten one of the most basic rules of sailing: if you want to turn left, push the tiller to the right. In a small sailboat she probably would have gotten it right. She would have been able to watch the angle of the rudder. But in Griff's huge ship the rudder was hidden from sight down under thirty feet of hull. To her relief the scraping sound stopped as the ship responded to the wheel and slowly swung to port. Nikki straightened her course and eased up her death-grip on the wheel as the ship floated past the end of the pier and out into the open ocean.

Fuzz and Athena joined her at the wheel. Cation pushed her way out of Athena's rucksack and scrambled onto her preferred perch on Nikki's shoulder.

Athena patted her arm. "A very good job of sailing, Miss."

"So," said Nikki, trying not to let her voice shake too much, "where exactly are we going?"

"ImpHaven," said Athena. "It is the ancestral home of the imps. Fuzz and I were both born there. It will be good to see it again."

Fuzz snorted. "It won't be like it was in our youth. I hear imps are crowding into it from all over the Realm. The anti-imp hatred that Rufius is stirring up has frightened them and they think there'll be safety in numbers."

"Yes," said Athena, "but it will still be nice to see it again. I haven't been back since I left home to become a King's emissary. My mother is still living there. It will be wonderful to see her again."

"Yeah, wonderful," said Fuzz in a distinctly unenthusiastic voice.

"Oh, do not start with your complainings," said Athena. "You will enjoy seeing her too. She doesn't hit you with her cane nearly as hard as Aunt Gertie does."

Fuzz just sighed.

"So how do we get to this ImpHaven?" asked Nikki. "Is it across the ocean?"

"No, Miss," said Athena. "It is not nearly so far. It is down the coast to the south, on the very edge of the Realm. It used to be a separate kingdom, ruled by the imps, but it was gobbled up by the Realm many centuries ago. Its main city, also called ImpHaven, is a seaport. So all we have to do is follow the coastline and we will sail right to it."

That didn't sound too bad, Nikki thought. She'd only have to turn the ship twice. Once to head down the coast and once when they reached ImpHaven. She decided not to think too much about how she was going to actually dock the ship at ImpHaven. Docking wasn't her strong suit, even in a small sailboat. During her sailing lessons on Lake Monona she usually chickened out when it came time to dock and just brought down the mainsail to let the boat drift slowly into the dock. Maybe she could do the same thing with Griff's ship. Anyway, they had miles of sailing ahead before she had to deal with that. She eased her grip on the wheel just a bit and watched the moon rise over the horizon as the ship slowly headed out into the wide ocean.

End of Book Four

Nikki's adventures in the Realm of Reason continue in the fifth book of the *Logic to the Rescue* series: *The Sorcerer of the Stars.*

The Logic to the Rescue series

Logic to the Rescue
The Prince of Physics
The Bard of Biology
Mystics and Medicine
The Sorcerer of the Stars

The Hamsters Rule series

Hamsters Rule, Gerbils Drool
Hamsters Rule the School

Excerpt from The Sorcerer of the Stars

Chapter One

---◆●◆---

Homecoming

"EVERYONE HOLD ON tight!" Nikki yelled, wiping the sweat off her face. The time had come. She couldn't avoid it any longer. They were approaching the harbor at ImpHaven and she was going to have to turn Griff's ship.

Everyone ran to the railings and wrapped their arms around the stout wooden posts surrounding the deck. Nikki checked the wind direction again. The wind was coming over the bow and the sail was luffing as the huge ship threatened to go into irons. If that happened the sail would be useless and they'd be dead in the water. She knew how to get a small dinghy out of irons. You just pushed on the boom and sculled the tiller back and forth until you got the sail back to a close-haul position. But with such a huge ship they couldn't possibly move the boom by hand.

Normally she would have tried to tack, but there wasn't enough wind. Tacking even a small sailboat required a fair amount of wind. Attempting to tack without enough wind would get the ship stuck in the no-go-zone, the area between the ten o'clock and two o'clock positions off the bow. Her only option was to try and ease the ship into a beam reach, with the wind coming over the side of the ship at the three o'clock position. That maneuver didn't require as much wind. Nikki glanced nervously at the sandy hills of the coastline. They'd left the Prince's dock in Kingston on a run, with a strong wind coming over the stern and blowing them straight out into the ocean. But during the night they'd slowly been blown closer and closer to the shore. She could now see the outskirts of ImpHaven and its cottages dotting the cliffs. Tiny white houses with thatched roofs. A line of windmills along the cliff top. A broad green river flowing into the ocean through two breakwaters made of rough boulders. Ships docked at a line of wooden piers just inside the breakwaters.

Nikki felt her stomach churn at the thought of having to navigate the narrow gap between the two breakwaters. She just couldn't do it. She wasn't skilled enough to perform such delicate maneuvers with such a large ship. Not to mention trying to dock it at one of the piers if she made it through the breakwaters without crashing. No, the beach was a better option. It was a long sandy beach just below the cliffs, and it was right off their port side. The ship might founder in the shallows as it beached, but that was better than crashing into the rocks of the breakwaters.

Nikki took a deep breath. She had to turn now, before the beach ended and the ship reached the first breakwater. She slowly turned the ship's wheel to the right, watching the mainsail closely. It flapped in the breeze, then the trailing edge of it caught the wind and the boom creaked as the ship slowly turned toward the shore. Nikki straightened out the tiller as the bow of the ship crashed through the first line of waves rolling toward the beach. Geysers of spray shot up from the bow.

"Darius! Fuzz!" she shouted. "Bring down the mainsail! Now! Cut the ropes if you have to!"

Darius the stonemason ran forward and slashed with his knife at the nearest rope attached to the mainsail. Fuzz waved at the other imps onboard and they swarmed up the rope ladders swinging from the mast and untied every rope they could reach.

The huge billowing mainsail slowly collapsed, like a balloon with a puncture, until it hung limply from the boom.

Nikki looked frantically from the mainsail to the shore. The ship was slowing now that the sail was down, but it still had too much momentum. The beach was approaching fast. "Darius!" she shouted, "See if you can drop the anchor! We need to slow down!"

Darius ran to the winch in the bow which controlled the ship's huge iron anchor. His heavy shoulders strained as he turned the handle of the winch. A creaking rasp sounded above the crashing of the waves as the anchor chain slowly revolved. Seconds later the ship gave a sudden jolt as the anchor caught on the seabed.

As Nikki suspected, the anchor didn't stop the ship. They were moving too fast. But the dragging anchor helped slow them down. The only thing left to do was to keep the bow headed directly toward the beach. Coming in broadside would tip the ship over on its side, but if she could bring it in straight they might be able to beach without tipping over. She tried not to picture what would happen if someone fell overboard and the huge ship crashed down on top of them.

Nikki tightened her grip on the wheel. "Darius! Fuzz! Everyone back to the rail! Hold on!"

The ship crashed through line after line of waves, slowing a little each time. Then they were through the last line of waves and Nikki felt a shudder as the keel scraped against the sandy bottom. The ship rocked and bucked like a bronco, but it stayed upright. Nikki thought they were home free until suddenly the rudder caught against the seabed and the ship tilted precariously to starboard. She struggled with all her might to straighten the wheel, but it was no use.

"Darius!" she yelled. "Come take the wheel!"

The stonemason staggered across the tilting deck, nearly falling on top of her as he reached the wheel.

"Turn the wheel to port!" Nikki shouted. "To the left! We need to straighten out our approach!"

The stonemason threw his weight against the wheel, straining to turn it. The ship continued to list to starboard. Barrels started rolling across the deck, slamming into the imps clinging to the starboard railing. But then a stray wave lifted the ship off the seabed for a brief second. Darius turned the wheel to port and the bow straightened. The ship righted and headed straight for the beach. Their speed slowed and the ship slowly ground to a halt, its bow on the dry sand and its stern gently rocking in the shallows.

Nikki sank to her knees in a puddle of sweat.

"Miss, you did it!" cried Athena, running up to Nikki and throwing her tiny arms around her. "You have gotten us safely to ImpHaven."

Nikki sat watching her hands shake as Darius threw a rope ladder over the side and the imps swarmed down to the golden sands of the beach. She felt like she was going to be sick.

"Here," said Linnea, kneeling down beside Nikki and digging into the bag of herbs hanging from her shoulder. "Valerian root. Chew it. It tastes awful but it will calm you down a bit."

Nikki took the woody, gnarled root and cautiously nibbled it. "Ugh. It tastes like old bowling shoes."

"What are bowling shoes?" asked Linnea.

"Never mind," said Nikki. She slowly got to her feet. Her knees shook as she tottered to the side of the ship and hoisted herself over the railing, climbing down the rope ladder like an old woman with arthritis. She splashed through the jade-green water and plunked down on the sandy beach, lying back and crossing her arms over her eyes to hide them from the bright sun. She'd been in more than a few tight spots on her adventures in the Realm of Reason, but sailing Griff's ship was the worst so far. So many lives had been in her hands.

It had been too much responsibility. Now she knew how airline pilots felt.

"Come on," said Gwen, sitting down on the sand beside her. "It wasn't that bad. You got us here safely, didn't you?"

Nikki didn't answer. She was wrestling with an overwhelming desire to rush back to the portal near Castle Cogent. To the gateway between the Realm of Reason and her own world. She wanted to see her Mom again. She wanted to go back to being an ordinary student at Westlake High School. She even missed Tina, the snarky captain of the Westlake debate team. The problems facing the Realm of Reason seemed to grow worse with each passing day and she suddenly didn't feel capable of coping with any of it. Not with Rufius, the wannabe-dictator. Not with Avaricious and Fortuna and their greedy plans which got people killed. Not with the Knights of the Iron Fist who were charging around in their steel-plated armor, bullying and harassing the citizens of the Realm. And not with the plight of the imps, who were being forced out of their homes by nasty people who didn't want them around.

Nikki squeezed her eyes shut as the first tears started to fall, but it was no use. Her whole body shook as she lay on the beach, crying silently. When she finally calmed down a bit she noticed that the beach seemed oddly quiet. She raised one arm and peeked out from under it.

"Everyone has gone, Miss," said Athena, who was sitting next to her on the sand. "We thought it best to let you have some time to yourself. Fuzz is leading them to my mother's house in ImpHaven. She has a large house, so there should be room for everyone."

Nikki sat up and wiped her eyes. "Sorry about the crying. I'm just a bit stressed out."

Athena reached out a tiny hand and patted her on the shoulder. "You cry as much as you want Miss." She looked at Nikki with pity in her eyes. "Do you want to go home, Miss? Because if you do Fuzz and

I will escort you back to the portal at Castle Cogent this very day. You have been a great help to us, but we will not keep you here if you do not wish to stay."

"No," said Nikki. "Well, to be honest, yes. I do want to go home. But I can't. Not yet. I want to stay here and help, if I can. Help fight Rufius, and especially help the imps. I don't know how much help I can be, really, but I want to keep trying."

Athena stood up and put her arms around Nikki's shoulders, giving her a tight hug. "Thank you, Miss. You are very brave to choose to stay in a foreign land and help people who are strangers. We are very grateful. And you have helped already, many times."

Nikki took a deep breath and got to her feet. "Well, let's get on with it then. Lead the way."

Athena nodded and started climbing the sand dunes which lined the beach. At the top a path wandered through the sea grass toward ImpHaven. It was hard work trudging through the rolling sand dunes, and the bright sun made Nikki wish that sunglasses had already been invented in the Realm. After half an hour of walking they came to one of the breakwaters which guarded ImpHaven harbor.

Athena walked a few yards out onto the breakwater and stopped to take in the view. At their feet green waves crashed against huge boulders covered with barnacles. Spray from the ocean waves misted their backs but inside the harbor the water was still. Steep hills surrounded the harbor on three sides. Winding cobblestoned streets twisted across the hills and led down to a small beach at the far side of the harbor. White-washed cottages with thatched roofs and roses climbing up their walls clung to the hillsides. Fishing boats painted yellow and royal blue bobbed in the water and tall-masted ships unloaded cargo at long wooden piers. The harbor was smaller than the one at Kingston but it looked busy and prosperous.

"It is a lovely city, isn't it Miss?" said Athena.

"Beautiful," said Nikki. "Is this the only imp city?"

"The only large one," said Athena. "There are a few small villages, but most imps prefer to live here in ImpHaven. Over the centuries our country has been slowly gobbled up by the Realm. It used to be much larger, but every year we lose a bit more land. The big people take our farmland, put a fence around it, and declare it theirs. There is not much we can do about it. The King issued a proclamation a few years ago making these land-grabs illegal, but people have ignored it." She sighed. "The King is a friend to the imps, but he is not good at enforcing his own laws."

A piercing whistle suddenly sounded from across the harbor. Nikki could just make out a tiny figure waving at them from the steps of a large stone house.

"That is Fuzz," said Athena. "He is only calling to us because he does not like spending time with my mother."

"Is that her house?" asked Nikki.

"Yes," said Athena. "It is the largest house in ImpHaven. She inherited it from her own mother. That side of the family is quite wealthy, by imp standards. We imps don't have such grand palaces as Muddled Manor and Castle Cogent, but we do have what you might call our aristocracy. At least, my mother likes to think of herself as nobility. Fuzz teases her about it, which is one reason why she hits him with her cane. The other reason is because he deserves it."

End of Excerpt

Made in the USA
Columbia, SC
20 March 2023

14070252R00086